Spoiled

Rhonda the Honda, as they lovingly referred to it, was no less than a bacteria trap. Sticks of fried potato littered the floor. Small coins, pen caps, and much-too-colorful blocks (made in the country of LEGO?) greeted me from the back seats. Did these people live without knowing about the invention of the trash can?

The female-child would not stop cooing and speaking to me like I was a baby.

And did she not understand personal space?!

Praise for **SPOILED**

"Kimberly will claw your heart
to shreds - but in a good way."
Susan Sempeles, author of
The End Is Not Happy

"Clever and delightful. *Spoiled* leaves me spoiled
wanting to read more of Kimberly's adventures."
Lois Thompson Bartholomew author of
The White Dove, a YA adventure.

"Pampered kitty Kimberly knew what everything
was worth until she lost everything and a girl showed
her where true value lies."
Melissa Sheperd,
author of *Savant*

"Awesome adventure tale…"
H A Berg, author of *Moonflowers*

"As an elementary teacher and children's librarian for 20+ years,
I can say this book follows a delightfully silly path to the heart
of the relationship between a cat and her person. A modern
setting for an 'aristocat-ish' story, *Spoiled* shows
that money can't buy, or replace, love."
Jackie Sisco

Spoiled™

BOOK 1

JAR OF
Lightning

ROB BADDORF

JAR OF LIGHTNING
Camp Hill, PA 17011
jaroflightning.com

ISBN: 978-1-956061-26-0
BISAC category code: JUV033050

Written & Illustrated by
Rob Baddorf

DEDICATION

To my loving family who
still laughs at my jokes.

And to God for not giving
me everything I "deserve."

Chapter 1

WHO WOULDN'T CHASE after riches if they had the chance? You know, daily visits to the spa, enough Siberian caviar to swim in, a few princess-cut diamonds as play-things.

Going back to that way of living is worth it. Trust me. Nowadays, a purebred with a pedigree as long as I have is hard-pressed to get even the basics: spreads of imported jams, Italian meats, and a French creamy brie—real cheese, mind you! You cannot call what I have suffered as "living." If you ask me, it was more like "doing time."

For example, take a deep breath through your nose. Let it linger. What do you smell? No, no, don't tell me. You probably still have yesterday's socks scattered on the floor.

I am on the seat in the back of a Rolls-Royce. Do you know what one of those cars costs? More than your parent's house, I'm sure. And what surrounds me is the intoxicating and musky scent of genuine leather—the real thing. You see, I have finally escaped—broken free of my shackles. At long last, I have escaped the lowly commoners!

Ahhh. This much leather gives me perspective. It reminds me of all that I've been missing. Mmm. Is that a hint of my new Madam's perfume? Mature. Classy. It smells like . . . like "expensive."

Oh, you would give up everything to have this life once you've tasted it.

What a relief it is to stretch out in luxury once again. Don't I deserve it? I suffered in the prison of prisons! ~~Is that a thing?~~ There I languished! Tortured by the lower classes and their petty way of living! Imagine eating nothing but a strict regimen of bone-dry nugget-sort-of-thingies for food. Drinking nothing but tap water (without even a lemon twist, mind you). And sleeping in a decrepit, nasty box. Made of cardboard. You must be cheering with me now for my escape!

And what about the villain who imprisoned me? A mean and cruel scoundrel at that. What do they deserve? Remember, looks can be deceiving. OK, what if I told you that in addition to being the bad guy, they were obsessed with the color watermelon-pink? Yes, I knew that would win you over!

Excuse me for a moment.

Where is my new Madam? And why is she taking soooo long?! Does she not know that I am *WAITING*? Hello!

Where was I? Oh, yes. While we must endure this delay, I will tell you a little of my tragic life. How fate ripped me from the lap of luxury and imprisoned me in the darkest of dark prisons. ~~Surely that is a thing, no?~~ Until today. Until right now—my successful escape!

Oh, and I shall tell you of my captor's demise. Her certain doom by something as puny as one piece of shrimp. And how no one can save her but me!

But I am getting ahead of myself. Let me go back to the beginning . . .

Chapter 2

WHEN I WAS BORN—no, no, when I graced the world with my presence—it was in a *very* different part of town. The part that most people rarely see. After all, it's usually gated. At least to the riffraff and the common folk.

The white-gravel driveway shot straight through the champagne-flute trees. The sculpted boxwood shrubs that lined the drive stood at attention. The birds sang a bit sweeter that day. Greek gods and goddesses announced my arrival.

In the east wing, I made my grand entrance. Apparently, I interrupted teatime. But the staff forgave my offense once they caught a peek of me. They used words like "adorable," "cherubic," and "sweet."

I will say, five other brothers and sisters joined me soon after. But I had been the first, which is worth noting.

Our mother, the saint, licked us each clean. With her smile upon us all—well, at least upon me—she closed her eyes for a rest. Her work complete, our dear mother, bless her soul, gracefully departed this world. The gardeners laid her to rest beside the award-winning tulip bed.

But sadness soon made way for the sun. At this time, the milk and honey flowed. ~~Actually, I don't remember any honey.~~ The maids and servants of the house doted upon us, hand and foot, like slaves. Our every desire was met. Play and laughter became the norm.

Once we had been weaned, the house servants busied themselves as the big day approached. The laughter ceased as combs whisked through our fine hair. Perfumes and powder drifted on the breeze. The servants adorned each girl with a ribbon and each boy with a little bow around the neck. All the while, the maids aligned us neatly in a row. Side by side we sat, with a chin lifted here and there when needed.

I first saw Madam as she descended the east grand staircase. She strode with an elegance much like Queen Elizabeth approaching her lowly subjects. Madam wore a silken white gown with a single string of champagne-colored pearls. Her hair was coiffed and crowned with silver and a tinge of blue. Madam stood before us, a vision of austerity and philanthropic beauty.

Sorry, I looked up "philanthropic," which means "a person who likes to help others." The word sounded big and important, but Madam was *not* exactly philanthropic.

"My, my," Madam said. "Such a fine display of beauty you all are." Madam began to pace up and down the line before us. "It is too bad there are so many of you. I can't possibly keep you all. One will prove to be quite adequate."

I stood up a bit straighter. All my precious siblings did their best to present themselves well. While others licked their paws and combed their fur, I fumbled about with at least a dozen different smiles before it dawned on me. A smile might not be the thing to win the day.

I tried to mirror my own appearance to that of Madam. I lowered my eyebrows to a state of disdain. I bent the corners of my mouth to a nice curve someplace between haughty and arrogant.

But did I have what it takes? To be smooth and swabbed? I mean *suave*.

Oh, if only Madam would pick *me*!

Chapter 3

WELL, WHO DO you think she picked?! I mean, really—can you say no to this sweet, adorable face? No, and neither could Madam.

Don't worry, Madam shipped off my siblings to other good homes. She boxed them up with velvet ribbons and gave them to members of her bridge club. But I had done it. I was her choice.

The important thing here is that I became Madam's one and only. Her favorite. But I knew there was more. Much more!

"Dear most holy God," I prayed, "who liveth in high heaven above, let me now receive what I so rightly deserveth . . . which is a lot, in case you didn't know. To start, I would like to be royally pampered—downright spoiled, if you must. With earthly riches and goods, and fine food, and luxury, and diamonds, and ungodly amounts of finery—oh, and a lavish bed (all to myself!) fit for a queen. Amen."

Needless to say, Madam doted on me with gold necklaces, bands of pearls, and diamond collars.

I orchestrated a team of servants all for myself. One to open and close doors behind me. Another to change the toilet paper after I had unspooled it for fun. One servant's sole responsibility was to pet me with long strokes from head to tail. I couldn't get enough. But when my fur was stroked, my—how should I say this delicately?—my backside lifted upward. I couldn't help it. Every time it happened, my rump would go arching skyward. Well, that low-class servant girl actually laughed, if you can believe it, and declared that I had a "butt elevator." How crass. Needless to say, I instantly ~~fired!~~ dismissed her.

As for my bedroom, I chose between the larger rooms in the west wing. If I felt like Egyptian cotton, I lounged in the Statler Room. If I wanted to roll around and frolic in the seamless silks from Bangladesh, I only had to pick the Armitage Suite. And naps—where do I start? The chaise lounge from India? Or atop the Ming vases? OK, those proved a bit tricky, but I only fell in twice, mind you. I had run of the manor.

At six o'clock every evening, I joined Madam at the Regency dining table. Seated twenty feet apart, I had to yell just to get Madam's attention. And trying to pass the salt? Forget about it! The nice thing was that I had my own crystal set close by. I liked my salmon poached and my greens steamed in water from the Himalayan glaciers.

"Now, now, Kimberly," chided Madam. "You should not play polo with your fondant potatoes. That's not very ladylike."

Indeed. Madam accused me often of not acting lady-like. I must have greatly disappointed her with my behavior, because not being very ladylike sure was a lot of fun.

I found plenty of fun elsewhere too. Madam collected shoes like there was no tomorrow. I liked to sniff through her collection. Valentino, Christian Louboutin, and many more names that I couldn't even pronounce. Some of my very best work occurred in Madam's closets. I can't remember how many shoes I clawed and chewed up. After all, I enjoyed helping make room for new ones. I know, it was my gift to Madam.

Many evenings, Madam would sit alone in the chancellor lounge and poke at her needlepoint. Her favorite stitchings were all of cats. Big cats, small cats—she filled the walls with hanging felines. I often wondered: if she enjoyed cats so much, then why did she only have one real feline companion?

One evening, I jumped up to join her while she stitched. I wanted to be close and for her to pet *me* rather than her others—the pretend ones. Purring loudly, I nuzzled up against the back of her hand.

"GAH!" Madam jerked her hand away. "Do not touch me, Kimberly! Bad kitty! Very bad."

Madam spent the rest of that evening washing her hands. Over and over she scrubbed them, building up the lather only to wash it away and start again. The whole time, she mumbled about germs or something.

I learned my lesson.

But every time a few raindrops appeared on the windows, I would lose Madam all over again. She shuffled off to her room, locking herself away. As the wind and rains blew, the servants and maids would tend to her. They boiled tea and heated up blankets, trying to calm her fears.

I don't want to complain. It really wasn't anything. But when the rains were at their fiercest and the winds were at their worst, no one ever came for me. I didn't like the thunder and lightning any better than Madam did. It sounded as if the mansion was collapsing around me. It sounded like the end of the world.

The best I could do was hide under the chaise lounge.

By myself.

Shaking.

I don't like those memories. I'm not sure why I would bring them up right now. Hmm. Maybe because it was the day after a particularly bad storm that I remember most vividly. A dreadful day I will never forget.

I had slept in. With a big yawn, I meandered my way down to the dining room. No Madam. I moseyed into the reading room, and then the east study. No Madam. Was she sleeping in late as well? Tsk, tsk. I marched up to Madam's bedroom. I enjoyed planning out the scolding that I would give her. I would start out firm. From there, I might move into a frenzied disappointment, only to end it all with a touch of indifference. A shrug, perhaps, like I didn't care.

"I hate to bring it to your attention, Madam . . ." I spoke more to myself than to anyone else. "But you have been getting up later and later these days." I pushed open her bedroom door, which was open a crack. "You are as bad at waking up as I am." I jumped up on Madam's eighteenth-century hope chest and then onto her Victorian bed, nearly drowning in the down comforter. "Maybe you should try Earl Grey in the morning. I'm afraid your herbal tea doesn't have quite the same umph that—"

I stopped. Staring.

"Madam?" I hesitated to touch her, knowing how much she hated it. But then I nudged her hand. It didn't move.

She didn't respond.

"Madam?" Again and again, I pushed her hand with my head. Harder.

Nothing.

Chapter 4

THE HOUSE SPILLED over with feet. Many more feet than usual, all scurrying about this way and that. Most of them wore shoes that looked downright cheap, if you asked me. And many of them marched about without looking where they were walking. The nerve! ~~And my poor tail . . .~~

I spent much of that time huddled under the chaise lounge. I cannot tell you how many teatimes there were when no one served me. How many naps were interrupted with the loud BANGS and THUDS of furniture being moved and dragged past.

What was happening to the world?! Where did etiquette suddenly go? And the basic need for a little decorum?

The one time I poked my head out for a little air, a set of hands snatched me. The next thing I knew, the Hands did the unthinkable. I am half-tempted to spare you the horror, but remember, I had to endure it, so I will spare nothing now.

The Hands took me outside. (Yes, for once that is NOT a typo.) Outside! The next thing I knew, I was planted in a cheap seat, next to a hole in the ground. I suppose sitting there quietly was supposed to be ladylike. So, I did. Where was Madam, after all? She wouldn't want to miss this. And why did these people put a beautiful, large box into the ground? Maybe Madam *did* want to miss this—there was so much dirt!

To be honest, it felt like sitting through one of Madam's operas. There were a lot of tears and wailing, and nothing really made any sense.

Afterward, the lawyers and accountants descended upon the house. Not far behind, a pair of cowboy boots, some wingtips, and a set of stiletto heels sauntered in. They all wanted to hear a reading of the will—whatever that was. I didn't mind the company. I continued rubbing up against one leg after another, but they kept kicking me away. How rude!

Yet, for all the talking the lawyers did, no one seemed happy. Cowboy Boots stomped about and then Stiletto kicked the ottoman.

The next day an auction took place. I steered clear of it all. They stripped the house stark naked. Where did my Egyptian cotton sheets go? The dining room table? Those barbarians would not take my chaise lounge, would they?

They could and they did.

Now, personally, I wouldn't mind skipping the next part of the story. What happened next was particularly shameful. But my humility, being as generous as it is, demands I tell it.

The estate held a yard sale for the little that remained. With the servants and maids long gone, the old gardener placed a few "odds and ends" on Madam's card tables. A blender, a hot water bottle, tarnished silverware, a box of *Sing Along with Mitch* records . . . The crowning jewel, neatly placed in a Longaberger basket, was an extremely attractive Siamese cat, whose name doesn't need to be mentioned.

Things could always get better. I smiled. After all, this was a second chance! I would find a richer Madam. The richest! My destiny lay in my own hands, or rather in my face. I frowned. I had charmed Madam—I could do it again.

The hot water bottle sold first.

Then a macramé owl.

One old ~~buzzard~~ lady even bought the basket I sat in. The nerve!

Were they all hard of seeing? Did no one notice me? Was I invisible? Like Madam, they would smile as they passed but they wanted nothing more than to keep me at a distance. Like a priceless artifact in a museum, set out to admire but not to touch.

Eventually, the gardener crossed out my selling price and lowered it.

After being lowered two more times, the word "FREE" appeared.

Then "FREE WITH RECORDS."

That was the low point. I will not try to hide it. But it was also the moment when I saw her. She had silvery-white hair and a glorious display of wrinkles. Was that a mink stole around her neck? And pearls. Indeed, real

Akoya pearls graced her pillar-like neck. This was the one. If only I could get her attention.

Another face suddenly sprang up right in front of mine.

"I tawt I thaw a putty tat."

"What in the—" I managed to spit out.

It looked and sounded vaguely like a child. Maybe eleven years old, and quite disagreeable, I might add. This girl sprouted more freckles across her face than she should have. That and she wore a gangly metal contraption on her teeth. Was this the result of poor breeding? It didn't look like exotic jewelry, mind you. I should know because she stood practically nose to nose with me. Ick.

"I did. I did see a puddy tat!" the girl said with an evil grin.

As you can surely relate, my heart stopped. My life with Madam had not prepared me for such horrors, such a vulgar display of cheer and mirth. I did the only thing any decent and civilized cat should do. I swatted her.

The girl-child yelped and backed away. At least long enough to give me the chance I needed. I batted my eyelashes at the rich lady and gave her my very best discerning frown.

The rich lady edged closer. Lifting her lorgnette glasses to her eyes, she gazed upon me.

"What a charming little kitty you are," she cooed.

What good taste she had!

"You look like you could use a good home," she said, reaching into her Gucci handbag. The amount of money that I spied in it was staggering. Enough to wallpaper the Taj Mahal.

"She does need a good home," a squeaky voice interrupted.

The human-child creature jumped in front of my elderly savior. And with both of her ~~unwashed??~~ hands, she grabbed me.

"MY home!"

I wanted to die.

And for good reason, I soon thought I had.

Chapter 5

Heaven help me.

Rhonda the Honda, as they lovingly referred to it, was no less than a bacteria trap. Sticks of fried potato littered the floor. Small coins, pen caps, and much-too-colorful blocks (made in the country of LEGO?) greeted me from the back seats. Did these people live without knowing about the invention of the trash can?

The female-child would not stop cooing and speaking to me like I was a baby.

And did she not understand personal space?! If it doesn't frighten you too much, I will explain. This child delighted in rubbing her nose on my belly. And if that wasn't bad enough, she then would blow against my belly and make an unmentionable sound.

I scrambled away from the clutches of the child long enough to watch as Madam's grand estate drifted away. It shrank smaller and smaller before the girl's ~~nail-bitten~~ hands yanked me away again.

A disagreeable name matched the disagreeable child: Signey Mary Taylor. Her name was Scandinavian and pronounced "scene-yay." But since most people could only butcher it, her parents finally gave in and called her "sig-knee" as well. Strange name aside, I could see that Signey must have been dropped as a baby. Her energy levels bounced between full steam and dead stop. Her choice in apparel created a fascinating study in poor taste. And oh, the pink—I don't know if the girl was trying to drown in it or if she was color-blind, but she needed to learn the concept of moderation. She also struggled to keep her hands to herself. If they weren't swiping her phone or in her mouth, they were on me.

I need to give the girl *some* credit. Signey showed admirable qualities as well. She knew a good photography model when she saw one. The girl took enough photos of me in the car to cover a dozen magazines. Signey showed me the screen for each one. If you asked me, she had a good artistic eye. Granted, with her beautiful subject matter, how could she go wrong?

When we got to the hovel where the child lived with her family, Signey gave me the grand tour. With a new burst of energy, the girl portered me around the house. I clung on for dear life. Into every room we went. Every bathroom, every closet, every nook and cranny . . . including the frightening cavern under their house she called a "basement." We had to see it all right then, didn't we? But the house was tiny. At first, it seemed little bigger than a shed. Perhaps there was an addition out back? But no. That was it.

After an achingly long day, dinner finally arrived.

Formal mealtimes are difficult to screw up. I was sure that Signey must own at least a ballgown or two to dress in. I myself took a moment to freshen up. My hope grew.

I was wrong. Signey *could* screw it up. She plopped down a bowl before me. On the floor, no less. A dish made out of plastic. Why was she hiding the fine china?

Then Signey came at me with a bag at least twenty times her size. The bag's gaping mouth could have swallowed me whole, but it stopped short. A mountain of something poured out. Landing half in the bowl, half out, it proved to be nothing more than dry sticks and pebbles. Was this part of the opening entertainment? Perhaps a lecture on ecology?

"Kimberly," Signey said, bowing as if she were the server at a French restaurant. "Dinner is served." A used dish towel dangled from her arm.

"Really?" I said. "Did I suffer the drive into the barbaric wilderness only for this?" I pawed at it. "Do you eat this yourself?" I put my paw down. "No. I will not eat this . . . this . . . *food*, as if you can even call it that!" I added a harumph for good measure.

"What's wrong, Kimberly? You have to eat if you want to grow big and strong."

"I will not eat *that*," I announced. "As a matter of fact, I will *never* eat again. Not until I have real food!" I could feel the passion rising up from within. My cheeks burned as I got louder. "Food from your table!" I began marching around the bowl with my head held high. "Hear me, child. On my solemn oath, I will not eat again. Not until I have classy food fit for classy arithmetic!"

I meant "aristocrats," obviously, but Signey was none the wiser.

"Kimberly, wait." The girl seemed genuinely concerned. Almost frightened. I could see in her eyes that she knew she had done something wrong. Good! I had her right where I wanted her. She was putty in my paws!

Signey ran to the refrigerator and began pulling out containers. With her arms spilling over, she raced back to my side. "What about this, Kimberly?" She sniffed the leftovers of a ham sandwich, nibbled it, thought about it like she was sampling wine, and then shoved it in my face.

I sniffed it. "Disgusting," I grunted, turning away. "Next."

After the same thing happened with a mysterious lump called "meatloaf" and a deviled egg (don't ask), Signey finally brought out the good stuff. Shrimp. I knew shrimp. Finally, the meal that I wanted and deserved sat before me!

"First you have to peel off the shell," Signey said as she demonstrated. Did I grow up in a barn?! Trust me, I *knew* how to eat shrimp.

"Then you pop it into your mouth like this."

"Hey," I barked. "Why not put that into *my* mouth?" I waited for her to peel another shrimp, but Signey didn't. Instead, the girl sat back and started to finger her throat. Her lips began to get puffy and swelled up fat like the butcher's fingers. She struggled with her breathing. It became raspy and restricted. Her face turned a shade of blue, which was complimentary to her pink outfit but didn't look exactly healthy. Her mother ran over. Assessing the situation, she had Signey lie down flat on the floor while the father dialed 911.

"Not to be rude," I said, leaning in, "but is this a bad time for someone to peel me a shrimp if she's not going to be eating it?"

To use one of Signey's own words, her health got a bit "sketchy" there for a bit. But the paramedics arrived just in time to stab the girl in the leg with an EpiPen. Apparently, stabbing her in this case was actually a good thing. And within the hour, Signey sat before me, tired but nearly back to her former riot of color and self.

I wept as I watched her parents clear the house of all shellfish. All that blessed food went straight into the trash. That is when Mother handed both of us steaming bowls of something that she called "mac and cheese." It smelled heavenly and, if I can trust my discerning taste buds, was likely an expensive dish only served to royalty.

I nibbled at it. Not bad. Alright, to be honest, I couldn't help myself—I wolfed it down.

I had seconds.

~~And thirds, but they were small.~~

Maybe living here with this Signey girl would not be so bad after all. Maybe more pleasant surprises awaited me. I could hope, couldn't I?

No, I didn't dare. I didn't like surprises. I didn't like change. I deserved more than this, didn't I? For all I knew, someday I might discover that this noble feast of "mac and cheese" was low class—a lie. And for that matter, Signey too. I swallowed one more thing that night: hope. If I ever had the opportunity to escape with a real Madam—a rich one—I would.

"Dear God," I started off. "What have you done?! What happened to my life of luxury and queen-like pampering? Hello? Please fix this ASAP! I think we both know it wasn't because of something *I* did wrong that this happened. So, I don't want to point a paw, but have you fallen asleep on the job, huh?"

I made another vow. Just like Madam, I would not let these people—the Taylors—touch me. I mean, on the inside. Deep inside. I would shut them out. Keep all of them at arm's length. Just like Madam did to me.

Especially that Signey girl.

If I let her get too close, who knew what I might catch.

Chapter 6

EXHAUSTION OVERTOOK ME. Fate had yanked me away from my Madam. It ripped me away from her luxurious estate. Fate humiliated me through a yard sale, which, by the way, will never be mentioned again. And now, an urchin had made it her focus in life to torment me.

I wanted my bedroom suite. And I wanted it now.

"I'll suffer with this one, if I must," I said. "I normally would not settle for anything as small as a queen-sized bed. But it looks like push has finally come to shove . . ." I nestled in and closed my eyes. But to be honest, the cotton sheets felt sandy (Or at least, like what I imagined gritty sand would feel like—it's not as though I would ever set my delicate paws on the beach.)

"Kimberly, you silly thing," Signey said as she dragged me away. "That is my parents' bed!"

Silly me, indeed. I knew there must have been something bigger. Better. Signey carried me to her own bedroom and plopped me down. What was this? A footstool?

"Kimberly, how about you sleep with me in my bed?"

A laugh escaped my lips. Signey called this *thing* a bed? It carried pens and pencils, and paperclips, and hairbands, and something spilling out of a bag labeled "cheese curls," and bookmarks, and even more junk I could not name or did not want to name even if I could. It was like trash floating in the ocean, adrift during a storm at sea.

I arched up onto my tippy toes. I could not make out what form of disease and world calamity lay beneath me.

The thought of it nearly made me ~~cough up a hairball~~ swoon!

"No, thank you," I managed to squeak and picked my way to the floor. "What are my other options?"

"Don't you want to share my bed?"

What?! Share it—ha! If you can believe it, this girl intended us *both* to use it. At. The. Same. Time.

I looked around. The floor under the bed had a similar appearance to the bed, only more dreadful. Darker. I shuddered. "I say we burn this bed and start over. Do you have gasoline? Matches? Have the servants do it."

Signey did not understand.

"There must be a place around here decent enough for me to sleep in." My sense of hope dipped. I yawned. I would have dropped asleep on the floor out of sheer despair, but a single pink sock stared back at me hauntingly. Signey's whole bedroom equaled one of Madam's walk-in closets. Where did the girl manage to put all her shoes?

Never mind, I found them. A pile of them teetered under her desk.

"I have an idea," I said. "What if I claw open a stuffed animal? I can form a makeshift bed out of the poor creature's stuffing and—"

"I've got it!" Signey's head popped out of her claustrophobia-inducing closet. The girl plopped something that looked like a shoebox down in front of me. "Kimberly, you can sleep inside my old diorama project. Sound good?"

Let's get something straight. The thought of sleeping inside of an old shoebox is repugnant to begin with. Only this shoebox had been, um . . . how do I say this? Decorated? Not with gold foil or marble, mind you. Think construction paper and crayon. The outside displayed what I believe were supposed to be flowers. A happy sun watched over them. It could also have been a person sick with yellow jaundice. I honestly couldn't say.

Signey reached inside the box. She ripped out a fistful of paper clouds and apparently the whole water cycle that had been glued inside. "Climb in! Give it a try."

For the second time that night, a laugh escaped my lips. And not the haha kind of laugh, you know. The other kind.

I lifted my nose. "I will gladly sleep inside of a dustbin before I sleep in that!" I used the word "dustbin," which is the British way to say "trash can." I thought it sounded noble. More worthy.

I marched over to Signey's trash can. I glanced in to see what might be in store for me. As fate would have it, a half-eaten tub of raspberry yogurt awaited. And if that wasn't bad enough, the insides were also littered with about a million hole-puncher dots.

"You don't want to sleep in the box?"

"No, I do not." That was my cue. I needed to make a point. If you make a vow, no matter how rash, it's important that you stick with it. With my head held high, I leaped ~~like a ballerina~~ into the trash can.

I didn't know at the time just how long the yogurt had sat there. Apparently, yogurt needs to be refrigerated. When I plunged into the warm and squishy center, it let loose a squirt of —how do I want to say this?—*aromatics*. Fine. It stunk to high heaven. Happy? It smelled like a creature that had died a thousand deaths. Amidst a raspberry patch, mind you.

And as for the paper dots, an eruption occurred that rivaled Mt. Vesuvius. The plume of white circles created a snowstorm inside Signey's room. I could barely see through the whiteout.

As for me? I survived, if that is what you are wondering.

I had made my point. I did not give in, and that was an accomplishment. I felt proud.

Granted, it looked like the trash can had tarred and feathered me. First in a pink, sticky goo and then with a nice coating of white polka dots.

I also received my first bath that night. Up until then, I had always washed myself, thank you very much.

And yes, baths are simply straightforward evil. There is nothing redemptive about them. If we didn't burn the bed, then we surely should have burned that blasted tub. ~~Remind me to look into that.~~

I shall skip over bemoaning the dreadful bath, as well as some of the words that Signey spoke of me while I was trapped in the bathtub. Oh, bother. Suffice it to say she called me a "drowned rat." How's that?! She couldn't stop laughing. I shall not forget such an insult. Enough said.

In the end, after Signey tried to make amends by using a warm towel (straight from the dryer, no less), things calmed down a bit. While the girl brushed her teeth in the bathroom, I snuck a trial run with the shoebox.

I am probably the *first* cat in the history of the world to actually climb into an empty box. Who knew that cats might take so well to it?

I'm almost ashamed to say it. But after all I had been through, it was the closest thing that felt like home!

Chapter 7

I SHOULD NOT have said "home." Yes, I found the box bed passable. But the next few weeks were rough. And no, I don't mean rough like my tongue. I mean rough like throwing a dinner party and realizing that you are out of silk napkins. Like serving filet mignon overcooked!

Let me illustrate.

Lip gloss. It shouldn't be cause for alarm, should it? Only things are never that easy when you are dealing with the lower classes.

Signey needed lip gloss. Apparently, it became a three-bell alarm. She ran around like a cracked-lip tsunami had crashed in on her. The desperate need for a swipe on the lips overcame her.

Only, her Very-Berry Blue lip gloss wouldn't do. And the Minty-Gloss Green one didn't seem to hit the spot. It had to be the Juicy-Watermelon Pink.

Mind you, I didn't care about any of this. I *needed* my third nap of the day. Beauty sleep, you understand. Required. But with Signey's rampage, I could not get even a moment of quiet. Signey plowed through her room looking for this flavor or the next, tossing clothing and toys in her wake.

I rolled over and began cleaning myself when Signey disappeared. At last, some quiet. But no. Moments later, she tiptoed back into her bedroom.

And she was quiet.

Too quiet.

I made the mistake of leaning over to see.

Signey clutched a big bag to her chest. Her mother's purse. She peered into it. Then Signey's hand slipped inside and began routing around. The bag wasn't a Gucci. That I know. The bag dwarfed Signey. It was large enough to carry half of Madam's library or maybe a dead body, which is probably what Signey's mother used it for. The library part . . . not the dead body.

Signey must have forgotten her desperate need for Juicy-Watermelon Pink lip gloss. She fingered and examined each item from the purse. A retractable ID badge. A pack of scented tissues. Gum. A compact mirror.

But the stick of pink lipstick brought her back to herself. And it apparently made her lose her mind at the same time.

Signey popped up off the bed like a champagne cork. Before her full-length mirror, she stuck out her lips. This had to be the first time this girl had her hands on makeup, because she did it all wrong. Nothing like how Madam would have done it, neat and petite. Signey's lips protruded like a duck. And she colored them with the elegance of a pirate swabbing the deck.

Hair spray followed. Ack! COUGH, COUGH, the smell!

Then eyeliner. If Signey wanted an emergency landing strip for airplanes, then she succeeded. Otherwise, she needed a bit more finesse.

I rolled over and yawned. Now, where did that nap go?

Listen, it was *her* face. Maybe it was Arts-and-Crafts on-your-Face Day, I don't know. I had no need to stop her.

But that's when I heard her call my name.

"Oh Kimberlyyy . . ."

Dinner? Already? Could sushi be on the menu just once? At least a girl can hope, so I rolled back over, excited, my eyelashes all aflutter.

"How would you look with a little makeup, Kimberly?" Signey said, approaching my box bed.

By God's grace, Madam never declawed me. SCHWING! Out came my defense. I decided right then that I would go down with the ship. I would defend my honor no matter the cost. To the brink of my nine lives and beyond if necessary.

But Signey knew some form of karate. Or dark magic. Before I could take a swipe at the child, she grabbed me from behind.

First of all, I noticed how good I looked in the mirror. I know that isn't very humble, but it needed to be said. Secondly, I do not like pink. And I do not want to speak for the color pink, but I don't think it likes me, alright?

Then it began.

I watched on in horror as Signey smeared that stick of hideous color over my mouth. It felt slimy and disgusting. I jerked my head left and right, trying to get away. I squirmed and fought helplessly. My efforts only dragged the pink marks longer, wider.

Signey paused suddenly.

She turned to the mirror.

I turned to the mirror.

The horror. I wore a disturbing smile. Ear to ear. No, literally. Freakish and—

Signey giggled. That mean-spirited, no-good child actually laughed!

In a mad flurry, I thrashed about, putting all my energy into slicing the girl to ribbons. Unfortunately, I still could not touch her.

That's when Signey's mom walked in.

Signey swallowed her laugh. ~~I wish she had choked on it.~~

"Signey, what are you doing?!"

Signey's mouth opened but her mother wouldn't hear it. She grounded Signey for a week. I petitioned to extend it, but of course, who listens to me? Halfway through the scolding, Signey burst into tears. Then, believe it or not, Mother softened. She fell for them. Mother sat down next to Signey and put an arm around the girl's shoulder. Pardon my French, but "Sucker!"

I marched back to my bed. I knew a faker when I saw one. No thank you. Crocodile tears.

"Now look at me." I ~~pouted~~ said. "How am I supposed to clean my face, thank you very much?! Does anyone here understand how hard it is for a cat to clean their own face? Much less when it's covered with something so pink and so sticky?"

I had to ask . . .

The next thing I knew, Mother tossed us both into the tub. Again! And with water. Like, liquid wet water. Again! And bubbles that kept popping in my face. Stupid pink ones at that!

Signey ended up giggling. Again. I honestly think she has problems. She came at me with a big, fluffy towel.

"No, do not touch me! I will slice you into a thousand little—"

She did not listen. But that towel—it was sooo fluffy and warm. Straight from the dryer.

"Let me wrap you like a snuggly, squishy burrito, Kimberly."

I was going to complain and say, "How about a French crepe instead?" But I didn't. Signey would never understand. I vowed right then that I would never *ever* take another bath, or be given a bath, or be generally near the bathtub—never ever again.

Signey pressed her forehead against mine. Eye to eye with me, she said, "Kimberly, I wouldn't trade this for the world."

I would, thank you very much. But being a warm, squishy burrito did seem to make things better.

But only a little!

Chapter 8

SIGNEY DID NOT hold the position of oddball alone. Center stage, perhaps. But not the only one.

For example, when Halloween approached, the rain and cold settled in. Signey hit a spell of boredom. It crept in through the cracks. Bad enough that it often caused her to lounge on the sofa upside down. I'm not making any comments about that except . . . it didn't seem very lady-like.

"There's nothing to do," Signey moaned.

"Why don't you bake a cake?" Mother suggested from the other room.

"Or you could rub my belly," I added.

"Noooo," Signey groaned. "I don't want to do that. I'm bored. What else can I do?"

I moved closer to her and straddled one of her lifeless hands. "You could move your fingers back and forth."

Mother said, "Why don't you read a book? Or better yet, you could start on your math homework."

"Mooommm! I'm bored, not insane."

"Back and forth, please."

"I want to do something!" Signey added.

I tried to make it easier for her. I squatted down a bit lower. "There, you may begin on my belly now. I can't make it any easier than that."

"Why don't you invite Terri over and work on your Halloween costumes?"

I interjected. "Any time now to rub will be fine."

"We already did," Signey replied. "We're going together as cops and robbers."

"RUB MY BELLY!" I didn't mean to yell. But it sounded like a good idea to me. Call it desperation if you want, but I flopped down on Signey's hand and scooched back and forth. I merely wanted to show her how it was done.

Mother interrupted. "Do you have a costume for Kimberly?"

Now, what would cause a grown woman to ask such a question? I had no plans of going. Actually, I already had plans for that evening. A nap.

But a light ignited in Signey's eyes. Without even one ounce of belly rubbing, the girl cartwheeled up onto her feet. Then she grabbed me.

Terri came over. Or should I say wheeled over? She arrived with her own chair. It had wheels on it. Big ones and small ones. I didn't understand, since Terri could not have been any older than Signey. Madam had a friend she would play bridge with who sat in a similar chair. Madam's friend could barely push the set of large wheels to get to the ladies' room. Not Terri. She zoomed about the Taylors' house like a wild stallion. When my tail faced certain separation from my body by one of her careening wheels, Terri merely leaned to one side. Half of her chair lifted and hopped over my tail. The wheels never even touched me.

Finding a warm spot on her lap, I pleaded my case before Terri and she at least listened a little better than Signey had. But when she pet me from head to tail, it triggered my—umm—backside to rise. "Kimberly has a butt elevator!" Terri gleefully exclaimed.

Someone had to defend my honor, so I spoke up. "I will have you know that the—I can't even say those two words together—that reaction you are so *fondly* referring to is very natural and normal for cats. I honestly don't see why such a vulgar name has to be applied to it."

The girls laughed ~~at my expense~~ and snipped away at their construction paper. The air smelled of glue and paste. Glitter drifted about and flashed in the late sun.

The girls gave me plenty of attention. I didn't mind that. At first, they made me a costume to look like a popular machine. BB-7. Or was it 8? Either way, it ~~made me look fat~~ didn't highlight my good side.

Next, I became Elsa from *Frozen*. Not bad. Not bad.

As a joke, Terri put a construction paper carrot over my nose. I did not find that funny.

The mermaid costume didn't do anything for my hips. And I honestly don't know why they would make me into a pea pod. Or a witch! (No comments, thank you.)

In the end, they dressed me as I rightfully deserved— as the queen of Sheba. Both girls ditched their own costume ideas. Even though Halloween took place outside, they carried me everywhere. On a red satin pillow, no less. And having cut palm branches from Father's office palm, they fanned me continually. For two hours, the girls treated me like royalty, like a queen.

Which wasn't half bad, I suppose.

Only, I never got my belly rubbed. I'm just saying . . .

In early December, Signey's father scared the life out of me.

"Kimberly, wanna help with a surprise for Signey?"

I opened one eye. We weren't exactly in the habit of talking. "What's in it for me?"

The next thing I knew, he placed me in one of the back seats of the minivan. Next to Stuart. Stuart was the eleven-month-old who spent most of his time behind bars. ~~Foreshadowing?~~ He didn't talk much. How could he when he mashed four fingers into his mouth at the same time? He hovered above me in his booster seat. With as many straps as it had, his seat would likely survive the end of the world, along with cockroaches and those cheese puffs. Stuart liked to stare. His eyes fixated on me. ~~My beauty?~~ Like I was the fly in his ~~cold cucumber soup~~ Cheerios. That child never blinked. Always staring. Always sucking.

"I don't remember saying yes," I growled at Father. Where were we going? And why me? Were naps carefully planned into this outing? Snacks? "And good golly, does no one ever clean out the crack of this seat? Hello? Does no one see this hairy french fry?!"

Then it hit me.

I had been duped. Hoodwinked. I had fallen for the oldest trick in the book.

Father had kidnapped me! He was dragging me to the worst place in the world. A place of murderers and killers! ~~Is that the same thing?~~ I don't even dare speak the name of it aloud. The three scariest letters in the cat alphabet:

V. E. T.

Chapter 9

FATHER TURNED THE minivan keys. Rhonda the Honda's engine rumbled to life. But then it sputtered, coughed, and died.

"Let me out!" I scrambled up with my two front paws on the side window ~~with the grace of a ballerina~~. "Somebody do something! I'm about to get SPAYED!"

Father turned the keys again. He pumped the gas, trying to keep the engine from stalling.

The neighbor turned and looked. He paused from stapling icicle lights onto his gutter.

"You! Fine gentleman," I lied. "May I have a word?" I yelled out of the crack in the window. The neighbor hesitated and wiped his sweaty forehead. Shaking his head, he began to waddle down his step ladder. With a belly as large as his, ~~why not throw himself off the ladder?~~ it took time.

"Car problems?" he asked as he approached.

"Yeah," Father replied. "I need to take it into the shop, I guess."

"Looks like you have cat problems too," the neighbor said, pointing a chubby finger at me.

"I don't understand," Father said. "I'm taking her to the vet—I mean, to the beautician."

"AHA!" I cried. "Did you hear that? A Freudian slip! The truth is out. Catch that, huh? Huh?!"

"We're holding a Christmas party," Father continued. "This is a present for Signey, having Kimberly all dolled up. Made pretty."

"Pack of lies!" I screamed. I turned back to my savior. I stuck out my lower lip. "Have mercy on me, neighbor with the most generous belly." I assumed he honored it since he let the bottom part of it peek out from under his shirt.

I batted my eyelashes and thought charming words. Call it a superpower if you want. When I want to be cute and irresistible, I am capable of melting icebergs.

Father started the minivan. This time, Rhonda the Honda's engine ran with no problems. He shifted it into gear.

The neighbor leaned in close to me. He tapped on the glass with his fingertips. "Have fun, kitty."

"What are you staring at?!"

Stuart continued to drill holes in me. He had laser beams for eyes. Judging me—I could feel it. It wasn't very ladylike, but I stuck out my tongue at him. Then I hunkered down for a good self-cleaning. I needed to think.

What could I do? I could throw my body under Father's feet. No, that was idiotic. Plus, it might hurt. What else? I had to do something. Anything.

An idea.

I scrambled to the back of the minivan. Nearly hyperventilating, I breathed on the back window. I would claw out a rescue message. But what should it say?! *Dear sir or madam* . . . Too long. *Nearly murdered, call 911*? No, no. Keep it simple, Kimberly! *Some pig*?

"I've got it!" With one paw steadying myself ~~from Father's maniacal driving~~, I used the other to claw out the letters *h* . . . *e* . . . *l* . . .

I hesitated.

For the life of me, I could not remember how to write a letter *p*. Which direction does the big hump go? To the right? To the left?

I finished my writing: *helb*.

That's when I realized that the whole message had to be written backward. The car behind couldn't read it unless I reversed it. *Blast it!*

What was *helb* backward? *Bleh.* Great. Just great! I spent all that time and told the world behind us of my total disinterest. Perfect.

I rubbed out what I had written. As I went to steam up the glass again, the minivan came to a stop. I rolled back toward the front ~~like a ballerina~~. Foiled again!

SLURP, SLURP. Stuart continued to stare at me.

"WHAT?!"

The disturbing child kept smacking on his half-digested fingers.

"Was that a smile, young man?" I leaned in and whispered. "'Cause if you don't wipe that smile off your face, I will claw it off faster than—"

Father interrupted, whisking me from the minivan.

The sign read PETCARE.

Care for pets, HA! The sign should have read PET BUTCHERS.

Fine. If they wanted a fight. I would give them a fight. SCHWING! Twenty-five beautiful claws popped out, ready to do their worst.

Sorry, I only have twenty claws. ~~(Had to count.)~~

Either way, I attacked Father. Slicing his hands.

"OWW! Kimberly, what is wrong with you?!"

I didn't let up. If anything, I went even more wild panther on him. I scratched and clawed. Every square inch that he made available, I took advantage of. He dropped me. I landed on all fours, ready for more.

"Don't play dumb with me, mister! I wasn't born yesterday, you know."

"Kimberly, this isn't going to hurt," Father said as he tended to his open wounds.

"What? Is that from your experience getting DE-CLAWED?!"

Three assassins in lab coats joined Father. They cornered me, those cowards. I hissed something terrible. If I had to take them on all at once, then so be it. Attack the weakest one. I'd start there. After that, I'd work my way up the food chain.

But who knew they weren't playing fair? A skinny lab coat snuck up behind me and grabbed me.

My goodness—he had an absolute iron grip and gloves three inches thick.

Into Petcare I went, kicking and screaming . . .

. . . ~~like a ballerina.~~

Chapter 10

To MY SURPRISE, Father had been telling the truth. Who knew?

I didn't get anything ripped out of me. Or off of me either. Instead, they made me beautiful!

Don't get me wrong, I radiated beauty when I arrived. But they enhanced it. I exited even more beaming than before. A vision of charm and refinancing.

Refinancing? Is that right?

What I'm trying to say is, I looked AMAZING!

Petcare combed me and trimmed my fur in a few spots which won't be mentioned. One staff member puffed me with expensive perfume. Only the best, mind you. And with a cleaning, nails clipped, and a classy bow for my head, I marched out to Father with my head held high.

Of course, Stuart did nothing but stare. Did his stern, unchanging judgment of me soften? Maybe he had a touch of awe and wonder? Either way, he knew when the presence of a goddess was nearby.

Father reached over to pick me up.

"Don't touch," I hissed. "I do not need your grimy hands on *this* body. Thank you."

Instead, I strolled behind him to Rhonda the Honda. Father at least had the decency to open the door for me, offering a little bow in the process. And as if that man couldn't be more polite, Father even brushed off my seat. Hairy French fry and all!

I situated myself for the royal carriage ride home. Father started the minivan. Or tried to.

GRrRRRrRR.

Finally, the engine coughed to life.

As we motored toward home, I had the urge to see myself again. After all, you can't let this sort of beauty go to waste. I leaned up on the front seat. I had to fidget to get a good view. That's when I saw it. No, not my stunning good looks—the rain. A few drops splattered the windshield. No bother.

Now, back to that beatific vision in the mirror . . .

Except, that is when the sky broke open. Rain dumped. It was like Father had driven into the bathroom shower. The windshield wipers swished back and forth, but they could barely keep up with the torrent.

And then the minivan SPITTED and SPUTTERED and died. Father cranked the engine.

GrrRRRrRR . . . it wouldn't start.

The jerk behind us had the nerve to HONK!

"Listen, buddy!" I yelled. "Give him a break! He's trying!"

Mr. Jerk zoomed past us as Rhonda the Honda drifted to the side of the road. Ka-TINK, Ka-TINK, our emergency lights blinked on and off.

"Who votes for visiting Petcare every week?" I asked to lighten the mood.

Stuart drilled holes in me. It was not that crazy of a question. After all, a girl needs a bit of pampering now and then.

GrrrRRRrrr . . .

"How about Petcare again tomorrow?" I added. "That too soon?"

Father turned and looked at Stuart. Then he looked at me. He sighed.

"Wait a minute," I said. "Why did you just sigh? What are you thinking?"

Father unbuckled his seatbelt.

"No, no, no . . ." I shook my head. "You don't have to go out there to fix the car. Someone will surely be by soon and will stop. Let them do the ugly manual labor of fixing the—"

Father interrupted me by opening his door. And holding a copy of *Architectural Digest* above his head, he climbed out.

Hello? Did he not see the pouring rain? I mean, what is a magazine going to do in a downpour like this?

Honestly, I don't blame the man for wanting to fix his car. But he didn't fix it. He didn't even lift the hood to try. Instead, he opened Stuart's door and unhooked his baby seat.

"My good sir," I spoke up. "I'm afraid your attempt to stay dry is sorely lacking when it comes to—"

Then Father turned his eyes toward me.

I stepped back. I mean, after all, the man had water streaming off him. And his hands were dripping water. Like moist, drippy, wet kind of water wet.

"Kimberly, I don't like this any more than you do. Come here. It's not far. We'll have to walk the rest of the way home."

I grinned. Surely this joke had gone on long enough, right? But Father never smiled back.

"Do what you need to do, my good sir, but I will remain here. At least until the rain lets up. From the looks of things, I can survive quite nicely off the bounty of dropped food around me. Feel free to come back for me this time tomorrow." My smile dissolved.

Getting spayed or having your fingernails and toenails torn out of your hands and feet is one thing, but this . . . this was another. I drew a line in the cracker crumbs. Father would not cross that line. Not if he wanted to keep his skin on! That's right. Not if he wanted to keep his major organs intact!

DING DONG! Apparently, Father had left the keys in the minivan, so he had to ring the doorbell.

Signey yanked the door open. Her Santa hat flopped to one side. "Merry Christmas! Welcome to—" Her face drifted from a happy smile to something else. Something dark and horrified. "What happened to you all?"

Father lugged in Stuart, who now swam in his car seat. He didn't seem any worse for wear. He still sucked his four fingers and crinkled his furrowed brow. But at least now, for once, his stare focused on his sister.

"Signey, Merry Christmas yourself," I grumbled.

Signey reached out and took me from Father. Water poured off me and my sopping bow, but at least I wasn't cold. Not anymore. My anger generated enough heat to keep me warm. Toasty warm.

Not long after that, Signey's school held a carnival. She bounded inside the house with a gaudy glowstick necklace, dancing about. A bag of cotton candy had wedged itself under one arm. But something sloshed about in her other hand. And that made me interested. *Mildly* interested, you understand.

"Look what I won, Kimberly!" Signey's smile scraped the ceiling ~~along with her blood sugar levels~~.

Signey thrust forward a plastic bag pregnant with water. Right in my face. I had to back up to get a better look at it. Tossed about inside of it was . . . was an orange blob.

OK, it wasn't a blob, but the hyper child could not for the life of her hold the thing still. She skipped back to her bedroom. The blob had looked orange. Or maybe gold. Hmm . . .

I didn't care what it was, honestly. "Cheap and trashy" came to mind. But then again, she won it. A prize she said. It could have been expensive. Wildly expensive. I didn't know. For all I knew, maybe it was an orange gem. Or a lump of solid gold! Hmm. Because it only takes a little ~~manipulation~~ work for it to become mine . . .

I followed.

GLUB
GLUB

Chapter 11

How DO YOU mount a lump of solid gold that size? No, no, you would melt it down first. Microwave? I couldn't help thinking about it. But why the water? Why did a priceless lump of solid gold come in a ziplock bag filled with water?

Did they run out of jewelry boxes?

Signey bounded over to her dresser. She grabbed the glass bowl she kept her generous button collection in and dumped the contents on her bed. No surprise there. The buttons had good company with the Real™ cheese curls.

(Just as an aside, how can a company legally call their cheese curls "real" when there is absolutely nothing real in them? Never mind, I digress.)

Signey blew out the dust from the glass bowl and then poured my prize into it.

"I would like you to move my incalculable treasure closer, please. Closer to my cardboard box if it's all the same to—"

The lump moved.

Correct me if I am wrong, but gold doesn't usually move, yes? I mean the 24-karat kind. I hesitated. Then I inched forward. I needed a better view. I leaped onto the bed, avoiding the fake mother-of-pearl buttons, then up onto the dresser.

I screamed.

Through the bowl, Signey's face greeted me, larger than life. And between us sat my lump of gold. Blinking. And making a kissy gesture toward me.

"Meet Fred!" Signey squealed.

A goldfish blinked back at me.

"Wait, wait . . . this is the prize? You actually won *this*?!" I blinked back at the orange blob in disbelief. I turned to Signey. "How exactly do you win something that costs as much as the ziplock it comes in?"

"I'm going to the store with Mom to get fish food!" Signey yelled over her shoulder. "You two make friends!" Signey grabbed a sweater and was gone.

I flopped down next to the fishbowl and groaned. The blank and meaningless ceiling somehow gave me solace. So much for having great riches again. Hope was officially gone. Why did I ever think the prize could be anything of value? My days of bathing in real gold were gone. Period. What a bitter pill to swallow. The riches I could hope for now came in plastic baggies. The irony. ~~(Like the cheese curls that contained *no* real cheese.)~~ And goldfish that contain NO real gold.

"'Ello there, mate," came a voice.

I leaned up ~~from my utterly bottomless depression~~ and looked around.

"You there, Kimmy Poo," said Fred.

"I beg your pardon," I said, jumping to my feet. "What. Did. You. Call. Me?" I leaned in. And to make my point clear, I shoved the fishbowl. Not much. Just enough to put it closer to the edge of the dresser. The fish had crossed the line. No one—and I mean NO ONE—called me cutesy names. I needed to make that clear upfront in case there was any confusion.

I tried to imagine what Stuart might sound like if he could talk. "My name is Kimberly," I said, drilling holes through the glass with my eyes. "Named after Queen Victoria Kimberly the Third. Or was it the Fourth? Never mind! Call me one of those other names again and you shall know my full wrath." I ~~snorted~~ breathed on the glass, steaming it up for effect.

"You mean like Sweet KimKim or Butt Elevator?"

I blinked, stunned. Did the fish actually say those words out loud?

I rammed the fishbowl, harder this time. Water sloshed about. Some spilled over the edge. The floor lay a long way down. I rammed the bowl once more. Half of the bowl now hung over the abyss. One more breath and this Fred character would learn to fly.

"They're only names I 'eard from the girl earlier," said Fred with a bit of a bow. "The girl said that you liked those names. At least, when the girl uses them while scratching under your chin. No offense, ma'am."

One of my eyebrows raised. Having your chin rubbed—and I mean *really* rubbed near the collar there— might be an exception to the rule. Of course, I would not tell the fish that. But I can forgive quite a bit when my chin is being scratched.

And did the orange blob actually call me "ma'am"?

Ma'am is short for Madam. At least Fred knew an element of class when he saw it. Maybe this fish wasn't all that bad. He did speak with a British accent. That had to be worth something.

"I shall forgive you this time, Fred," I said with my head held high. "But do not let it happen again. Ever!" I gave the classic head-turn-with-disdain and marched away. Or, I meant to—when my tail brushed ever so slightly against the glass.

The bowl slipped forward a fraction . . .

. . . and tipped over the edge.

Chapter 12

GOOD GOLLY, I am NOT a murderer!

I snatched the lip of the bowl with a paw. But that ~~fat~~ fish weighed as much as a grand piano. What did he eat? Real gold?! The bowl began dragging me off the dresser with it.

"Wheeeee!" cried Fred from inside his bowl. "This is fun!"

"Fun?!" I hollered as I scraped and clawed for a better grip. SCEEEECH! Little coils of wood snaked out from my nails. The bowl continued its descent over the edge.

"More! More! I'm flying!"

I arched back, pulling as hard as I could. My arm socket spontaneously ignited in flames. ~~Well, that's what it felt like.~~

"Shut up, you stupid goldfish! And flap your fins!"

Fred gleefully swam in circles. "Look! I'm a seagull!"

Inch by inch, he dragged us both farther over the edge. Given half the chance, that dumb creature would drag us both to our doom! I had to do something. Anything if I wanted to ~~keep my blessed manicure~~ be the hero.

With one mighty yank, I jerked at the bowl. It wasn't enough to level the bowl, but I did manage to swap out my paw for my teeth. I now held the lip of the bowl with my jaw while all four paws firmly gripped the dresser top.

You might think from all my naps that I never worked out. In this particular case, you would be correct. But that did not mean I have no muscles. I have muscles to spare! You should have seen me. I squatted like ~~an Olympic~~

~~weightlifter~~ a ballerina and got the best grip I could. Then I pulled.

Inch by inch, I hauled that blasted fish and his bowl closer to safety. Straining my mighty strength to the very limits, I pulled. (Though I would like it noted that I did not break a sweat. A proper lady never sweats.)

Pulling, pulling, I got that ~~obese~~ fish and his bowl back onto the dresser completely safe and sound again.

Almost.

Trust me, I could have done it. But that fish . . . oh, that fish. Why, oh why, did Signey have to win *that* gold-fish?!

"Until you spread your wings," Fred called out, "you've no idea how far you can fly!" Then he leaped from the bowl and nose-dived toward the floor.

The weight of the bowl dramatically changed. I was pulling so strongly that it suddenly went soaring over my head. It bounced off the wall and hurtled right back at me! I didn't even have a chance to duck. It bowled me over, spraying water this way and that, knocking me clean off the edge of the dresser.

Fred had the good fortune to land on a new bag of Real™ cheese puffs (which are *not* real). Signey had hidden it between her dresser and her bed. The bag acted as a trampoline, neatly planting Fred atop a fuzzy, pink slipper.

As for myself, I had no such luck. Though I did land on the same bag of not-real cheese puffs. I would also like it noted here that a real lady would never speak of her own weight. And I am a true lady. But I do feel the ~~absolute urgency~~ mild need to make an exception.

I DO NOT WEIGH MORE THAN THAT GOLDFISH! I must have landed funny, that's all. Something about my girlish figure proved to have a different effect on the bag of artificial-cheese cheese puffs.

It burst open.

A plume of orange cheese-product-stuff erupted into the air. It coated me head to tail in the process.

"Imagine that," Fred said, snorting a laugh. "I'm a bird and you're the goldfish!"

I glanced toward the full-length mirror. Indeed. I had become an orange blob. I could feel the processed grit grinding into my fur.

I had no time to clean myself, despite the nearly overwhelming urge. I could hardly leave the poor fish there to die! ~~Although I did think about it. For quite a while, too.~~ Fred only had seconds left. Seconds before he would run out of air.

How could I pick him up? And where could I take him? I had no hands.

Even if the world was about to end, the *last* thing I would do would be to pick up a dirty fish with my mouth.

What if I ran the garden hose through the window? For that matter, I could clog up the sinks and flood the house. OK, not practical.

"Never regret—thy fall, O Icarus—of the fearless flight," Fred said between desperate gulps for air. "For the—greatest tragedy—of them all—GASP—is never to feel—the burning light."

Great. I had to rescue a classically trained goldfish.

"Oh, fine!" I picked up Fred in my mouth. Gently and gingerly, mind you. Yuck, yuck, YUCK!

I went to the toilet first. And I would have deposited Fred inside the bowl *iffffff* the last person actually had the decency to flush.

"To die—to sleep," Fred coughed and wheezed. "Perchance—to dream . . ."

Drat it all! See, I can quote Shakespeare too.

I raced with Fred to my water dish. To be honest, I hesitated before it. If I did this, then I would never be able to drink from the ~~poisoned, icky, disgusting~~ bowl *ever* again.

Fred lifted a wilted fin over his forehead. "For in this sleep of death, what dreams—"

I spat out Fred. Probably more to shut him up than anything else.

Fred began swimming laps in my water bowl. "Perfect! I like it in here." He had returned to full health awfully fast. Hmm . . .

Car lights washed over the wall. Signey and her mom must have come home from the store, fish food in tow. Boy, did I have a story to tell.

I made my way to the front door to greet them. I awaited my hero's welcome. A medal, at the very least, for all that I had done. Maybe a bronze statue. Nah. A *gold* one!

Only it wasn't Rhonda the Honda outside.

A Rolls-Royce pulled to a stop in front of the house. The most expensive and luxurious vehicle ever made.

And out of it stepped a pair of Christian Louboutin heels. Only the most expensive and luxurious ladies' footwear ever made. I raised my gaze. An all-silk, all-white dress glided forward like a ghost. Even though the lady's hips swished back and forth, her head stayed perfectly still, like she balanced an invisible book on top of her platinum-blonde hair. I watched, mesmerized.

And believe it or not, the lady approached the Taylors' house. She approached *me*.

Who was she? And why had she come?

It didn't matter. *MY* ticket out of here had just arrived.

My new Madam.

She might not have known it yet. But I vowed right then and there that no matter what happened . . .

. . . she would SPOIL ME!

Chapter 13

THE LADY WALKED toward me with one hand held high, as if she was carrying a martini.

She approached the house. This house.

Wait a minute. Had she seen me in the side window?

I looked like an absolute wreck! WHAT COULD I DO?! I ducked but had to keep one eye there to peek.

Her long and slender finger pressed the doorbell like she might touch a germ. I counted six—yes—there were no fewer than six diamonds on her bracelet. Make that an even dozen if you counted the rocks wrapped around her fingers—wow. She slipped out a pencil-thin case and twisted it. Lipstick spiraled out. The darkest and deepest red (not pink!) I've ever seen. With one pass over her lips, they were colored. Magazine perfect.

I leaned back from the window. I couldn't let her see me.

Father approached the front door from inside the house. He peered out the side window and wrinkled his brow. His hand reached out to open the door.

But my legs wouldn't move. The artificial cheese must be hardening. ~~That, or my nerves.~~

I managed to spring back and hide behind the door just as it opened.

"Hello," Mr. Taylor said, clearing his throat. "May I help you?"

"I certainly hope so," said the lady as she pushed open the door and welcomed herself inside. "I am seeking out an Arthur Taylor, the architect. Are you he?"

She actually said "Are you *he*," and not "Are you him?" Did you hear that? That is refinement. I couldn't fight a growing smile.

"Why, yes. I am Arthur Taylor. And I do architectural designs."

Then the lady actually did the most daring thing. The most refined thing yet. Standing next to the end table that held the minivan keys and outgoing mail, she finger-swiped it. Then she studied her fingers. A discerning eyebrow raised as she rubbed away the dust and turned back to Mr. Taylor. "You could hardly be *the* Arthur Taylor who won the Pritzker Prize for his design of the Cavalier Building?"

She had me at the finger swipe. I wanted to melt. I did melt. I gushed. I blushed. I wanted to jump for joy and for the Greek gods to blast once more on their trumpets!

Mr. Taylor swallowed hard. He still hadn't stopped shifting his weight or drying his hands on his slacks. "I am. And who, may I ask, are—"

She cut him off as she handed over a thick business card. Expensive thick. Gold-foiled, I might add.

"I am Ms. Goldborn"—she pointed to her card with her pinkie finger—"as I'm sure you can read." She smiled, as thin and weak as the second use of a teabag.

Ms. Goldborn. That was her actual, glorious name! Can you believe it? I'm not making this up.

Mr. Taylor coughed politely. "If you would like to schedule a meeting at my office downtown during regular business hours, I'm sure I can—"

"I would *not*, thank you," Ms. Goldborn said. "But I would like to hire you right now. Do you have a home office where we can discuss the details?"

I freaked startled. I know that isn't very ladylike, but sometimes you have to do what you must. In a single bound, I leaped into the neighboring family room and slid behind the couch. Why did the couch look more awful than usual? And I didn't leave behind that orange trail of not-real cheese . . . did I?

"Um, yes." Mr. Taylor closed the front door. "Please follow me."

I stood on the bathroom counter, looking in the mirror. I frowned at my horrifying reflection. All thanks to Signey and her poor choice in pets.

I didn't have long.

Ms. Goldborn likely wouldn't likely stay for more than a handful of minutes, if that. And I needed to make a first impression. Not just a good first impression—a stunning one.

Especially since she was destined to adopt me.

I frantically licked at the cheese powder. YUCK GROSS BLECK! It tasted as nasty as it looked. I nearly gagged. I shot a sideways glance at the bathtub and re-membered my vow. There was no chance of my getting in there.

I licked and licked again. Too slow. Forget it. I didn't have forever.

I stared in the mirror. Great, now my tongue gleamed orange too!

Desperation.

Yes, *that* desperate.

The bathtub loomed out of the corner of my eye.

Was this really worth it?

I paused. Then I jumped in.

YAAAAAH! I screamed my mighty battle cry as I bat-ted and clawed at the water knobs.

Now, will someone tell me why the hot water has to be so blooming hot?

Ooo, OW, WOW! I danced about getting soaked, all while suffering for a good cause. Orange water poured down the drain. Hot, hot, HOT! I whacked the knobs again.

Cold. Cold. COLD!

Can someone tell me why they haven't invented a knob called "Just Right"?

I could barely stand to run back and forth under the terrible water. But every time I did, I watched as more bright-orange cheese powder washed off me. That gave me strength. Back and forth I ran. Back and forth. My teeth chattered away.

When the water ran clear, I thrust the knobs off.

Never again, I vowed. Never again would I take a bath. This time I meant it.

SO COLD.

I tried to jump out of the tub, but my legs would not work. They shook terribly. I balled myself up, desperate for warmth.

I lay at the bottom of the bathtub, shaking.

If only Signey would walk in. Rescue me. I had second thoughts, I admit it. Right then, I might have given up Ms. Goldborn for a simple towel from the dryer.

So cold. I closed my eyes. I wasn't going to make it.

Ms. Goldborn and Madam had much in common. So wealthy. So refined.

So cold.

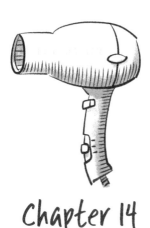

Chapter 14

EVERYTHING SLOWED. Became sluggish.

My eyes wanted to close.

A glimmer of light caught my attention. There on the edge of the faucet. It glistened brightly like . . .

Like a diamond.

Yes! The sparkle. The twinkle. I reached out for it. Where did it go?

I leaned up and found the strength to climb to my feet.

I needed the glitz and the glam. I clawed myself out of the tub. Wet but reborn.

I could be Ms. Goldborn's new diamond. Another shiny bauble twisting around her wrist. Even if I was still frozen.

Now to dry off. I climbed onto the toilet seat and then onto the counter. The hairdryer lay on the counter, still plugged in.

I had no time to waste. I batted at the set of switches on the blasted thing. ~~Pardon the pun.~~

I braced myself for the winds, yet I still nearly toppled off the counter. I leaned into the gale, turning my body this way and that. The hot air thawed me.

Mr. Taylor's voice drifted in from the hallway. They must be saying their goodbyes!

No time to primp in the mirror. I leaped down from the counter.

Before rounding the corner, I paused. I needed my game face. Stern and uninterested. A true lady never runs. I sauntered into the foyer. Ms. Goldborn spoke with her back to me.

"Don't disappoint me, Arthur," she said with a little artificial laugh. "Money isn't a factor, so give me something grand. Something that will win all new awards. Yes?" Ms. Goldborn spun toward the door, not waiting for an answer.

That's when she looked down. At me.

"AAHHHHH!" She recoiled and lifted a leg as if a rabid creature stood ready to bite her. "What is THAT?!" she exclaimed, jabbing her pinkie at me. "It's HIDEOUS!"

Needless to say, the impression I had been going for looked rather different than this.

Hearing the scream, Signey ran into the room. Even she hesitated. But only for a moment.

"Kimberly," she said as she bent over and picked me up. "What happened to you, love?"

Exactly. What *did* happen to me? Did I still have an overlooked spot of orange on me? Why were they staring at me ~~like I had used the wrong dinner fork~~?

Signey spun both of us around to face the hallway mirror.

Only what I saw in the mirror was not me.

Signey held a giant puffball. And it *was* hideous. Why did my face stare out from the center of it?!

"Unusual choice of pet," Ms. Goldborn scoffed. "If you can call that—that thing!—a pet. Anyway, I shall be going." She opened the door and sauntered out, not bothering to close it. "Do not forget my designs, Arthur. I shall return soon for them."

Signey held me in her arms as she sat on her bed. She combed my hair a hundred times in each area. It felt wonderful!

I grinned. My encounter with Ms. Goldborn had not gone to plan. But maybe it had gone better than I thought. Ms. Goldborn's reaction convinced me. How else would a lady of refinement and good taste respond? Like the princess and the pea, she had passed the test. I could not want more in a new Madam. She was perfect.

Wasn't she?

Signey leaned down. "I don't know what happened, Kimberly, but I'm glad you're alright. It looked like you licked the electrical outlet." Signey rubbed her nose with mine. "I never want to lose you."

"Dear God," I earnestly prayed. "Whatever it takes, please, oh please, let me escape this misery I suffer. Please let me escape with that lovely, rich woman. Someday very soon, please." I paused. "Pretty please!" I added, just to be extra sweet to God.

Signey interrupted my prayer and held my cheeks in her hands. She pulled me close. "You are perfect, Kimberly," she whispered. "I hope you know that."

Soon enough Ms. Goldborn would be back for her building plans. This time I would be ready.

I would NOT miss the golden opportunity right in front of me.

Chapter 15

I STRUTTED ABOUT the house a little lighter after that. The next morning, I leaped onto Signey's bed and from there onto the dresser.

"Good morning, Fred." I tried the friendly approach. I wasn't going to hold a grudge ~~even though yesterday was all his fault~~. "What's for breakfast?" I added.

But Fred could not be found in his bowl. In his place, a dollar-store castle poked up above the water level. And little pink stones (they had to be pink, didn't they?) littered the bottom of the bowl. Not to complain, but the castle wasn't winning any architectural awards. (I'm sure Ms. Goldborn would agree.) The castle had a ghostly white and slightly green hue to it. Did it glow in the dark? And the little pink rocks . . . God surely never created anything quite that ghastly or artificial. ~~Did God create Real™ cheese puffs?~~

Oddly, some of the stones drifted upward behind the castle. Then they settled again off to one side.

I tiptoed around the bowl.

On the far side, Fred sucked in the pink rocks and then spat them out.

"Morning, Miss Kimberly," Fred said between his efforts.

"What, pray tell, are you doing exactly?" I asked. "Aren't your efforts going to waste when you simply—"

"Shhh!" Fred hushed me. He looked about for anyone listening in. "Me and the boys are makin' a break for it."

"What do you mean 'making a break for it?'"

"We're digging, you see. If'n we dig long and 'ard enough, we'll be pokin' out the other side."

"The other side of what?" I bent my head down to see under the bowl. The dresser stopped me. *Naturally.*

"China, ma'am!" Fred said with a grin. "The other side of the world—imagine! We plan to escape before night-fall."

"Uh-huh . . ." I didn't know what else to say. This fish had issues. "Well, I wish you and *'the boys'* all the best."

"Mighty kind of you, ma'am," Fred said, tipping his absent hat. "We'll send you postcards when we arrive!"

Hmm, my comrade in prison. All the more motivation to run off with Ms. Goldborn. I would simply die if I didn't return to a life where there weren't such—how do I say this?—peculiarities.

~~Speaking of peculiarities,~~ Signey bounded into the room. Sweat beaded on her forehead. Her bright blue uniform displayed the number thirteen.

"Kimberly, guess how we did at soccer finals?" she said, holding something behind her back.

"How you did? Hmm. Let me guess . . . last place?"

"We WON!" Signey plunked down what must have been a dollar-store trophy. "We were only third place and—"

"Wait," I ~~was forced to~~ interrupted. "You got third place *and* you won? How exactly does that work itself out?"

"Look at this beauty," Signey said, pointing to her new lump of plastic she called a trophy. "I can add it to my collection."

Third place. And they gave her an award for it? That's like rewarding the peculiarities.

I don't know what overcame me, to be honest. Maybe the smell of the cheap plastic overtook me. Yes, I'm sure that contributed. I headbutted the stupid trophy. I didn't mean to. The part of me that can't stand hypocrisy did it.

The trophy took the dive this time. (Trophies made of real metal are not this easy to push over, FYI.)

SNAP! Off popped the head of the soccer person.

"I am soooooo sorry," I gasped. And for a change, I was. ~~Mostly.~~

Signey looked at her broken trophy splayed on the floor. In slow motion, she bent over and picked it up.

What possessed me to do that?! If they gave out trophies for losing, it really wasn't my business. I was fine with it.

Only I wasn't.

But I was, really.

The whole thing twisted in my belly. I felt sick. Like the lowly commoners themselves, made of plastic and fakeness and artificial cheese and glow-in-the-dark.

I wanted to run away but I stood my ground. I knew what was next. The yelling, the disapproval. I had seen it all when I had touched Madam. I looked at Signey and swallowed hard. I steeled myself, ready for the worst. Ready for the punishment she would give for my terrible, awful deed.

But Signey didn't react as I thought. She didn't react like she was supposed to. "I know it was an accident, Kimberly," Signey said. "I forgive you."

Then she smiled and placed the trophy back on her dresser in front of me.

Signey turned to her trophy collection. ~~All Dollar Store if you asked me.~~

Holding the base of one trophy—WHACK!—she knocked the head off it, using the edge of her desk, and laughed.

WHACK, WHACK, WHACK! Head after head rolled. Some knocked off more cleanly than others. Peculiar.

I didn't mean to destroy her well-earned prize. But here she was, beheading her trophies. Did she want them all to match?

A twang of pity rose up in me. Signey was certainly *peculiar*. Much like Fred. ~~And the rest of the family.~~

Maybe I didn't understand that word. I thought it was the polite way of saying that something was bad. Broken. No?

The least I could do was give a crumb of effort toward fixing this poor girl before I left her. Maybe point her in the direction of poise and civility. Or was she too far gone? Maybe all of them were.

Peculiarity surrounded me. I could drown in it here at the Taylors'.

Thank goodness I certainly wasn't *peculiar*.

Was I?

Chapter 16

I YAWNED.

I suppose that wasn't profound enough to mention. But since I've already mentioned it, I'll say it was a metaphor.

My life mainly consisted of sleeping, eating, looking out the front window for Ms. Goldborn, and snoozing. ~~Did I mention naps?~~

At her desk, Signey talked on the phone with Terri.

"On Dave Carvacho's, I wrote: 'Cheat off my test one more time and I'll tell Mrs. Romaine. Happy Valentine's Day.'" Signey laughed.

I rolled over.

"I don't know what to write on Jimmy Bolen's. I know, he's sooo cute! What?! You're kidding." Signey gasped. "Why would she do something like that? OK, bye." Signey threw the phone on her bed and ~~overdramatically~~ sighed. After a moment, she grabbed a piece of construction paper and stretched for the scissors. She cut like a madwoman. Bits of paper flew into the air and drifted to the floor.

I could have taken another nap, to be honest. But how do you turn away from a train wreck? And why are cats vexed with this problem? You know the saying about curiosity?

Not me, mind you. I only got up to investigate.

Mistake number one: don't show interest when it doesn't involve you.

Signey cut out a dozen heart shapes and busied herself with more scissoring.

"Guess what, Kim? Becky Kildare apparently mailed Jimmy Bolen a 'very special' Valentine's card." Signey grabbed the rubber cement and twisted it like she was finishing off the Christmas goose. "Which means Jimmy might have already gotten it."

"Are those pipe cleaners?" I had to say something. For the sake of art, if nothing else. "Goodness, girl, what's next? Dried macaroni?!"

Signey turned to me. "What if Jimmy gets her card before the official card swap tomorrow?"

"Maybe I should leave you alone." I tiptoed away. "With your artistic masterpieces."

"Kimmy, you have to HELP ME!"

"Ooookay." I spun back around. "Um, why don't we start with capping the glue. The fumes are beginning to—"

"Dear Jimmy," Signey scribbled on a heart. "Do you even like Becky Kildare?"

Signey crumbled the heart and threw it aside.

"Oh, boy. Signey, I think my best talents right now involve closing my eyes. But trust me, I will be listening. You do not have to worry about—"

Smiling, Signey grabbed a new heart. "Jimmy, do you like me? Circle yes or no." Her smile flipped. Signey ravaged the heart with her colored marker.

Another crumbled heart joined the first.

I lay down. A long night awaited us both. "No, no," I stifled a yawn. "That one was brilliant. Definitely my favorite."

Signey savagely cut out a new heart. Bigger must have been better.

"Can we go to bed?"

Apparently, bigger wasn't better. One more crumpled heart landed next to the growing pile of rejects.

"Let me rephrase the previous question," I said. "Can I go to bed and leave you to suffer alone?"

Signey grabbed her marker. "Oh, I have an idea . . ."

I laid my head back down.

I blinked. Darkness surrounded me. Had I fallen asleep?

"No, no." I stifled another yawn. "That one was brilliant. Definitely my favorite."

I looked around. No Signey.

Where did she go?

The curtains billowed from the wind. How did the window get open?

I leaped onto the back of the faded ~~pink~~ corduroy chair, then onto the bookshelf. I edged closer to the open window, trying to peer out.

"What are you doing?!" I yelled as Signey scampered down the latticework. "You're not allowed out at night, young lady!"

Signey looked up at me and mumbled something. Reaching the ground, she looked around. "I have to do this," Signey whispered up at me, having yanked the valentine from her mouth. "I have to slide this under Jimmy's front door. I'll be back."

"Oh no you don't. You climb back up here right now or . . . or . . ."

Signey slipped into the darkness.

". . . Or you are grounded!" I pounded a paw on the windowsill. Unfortunately, cat's paws are rather soft. "Did you hear me? Come back here right this instant. That's an ORDER!"

I paced on the windowsill.

"What if you get hurt? What then?"

"'Urt?" Fred blurted. He had just woken, and his eyes were still trying to focus. "Who's 'urt? We under attack?"

"Signey!" I barked. "She's gone out the window."

"She escaped? Through the glass? Why, that lucky—"

"For heaven's sake, Fred! She might already be bleeding to death! She could have been hit by a—I don't know—by a wild buffalo!"

I jumped onto the bedroom floor. Something had to be done. I jumped back onto the windowsill. "You could catch your death this time of night."

"'Ow exactly do you open the windows round 'ere?"

It all rested on my shoulders, too. Oh, the weight of the world! That rotten, no-good girl had done this to me! She had manipulated me. I did NOT want to care!

I jumped back onto the bedroom floor.

But I didn't care, right? I breathed in deeply, calming myself. I didn't.

RIGHT?!

I jumped back up onto the windowsill. I peered out into the inky-black night. The sound that drifted in through the open window sounded like a million crickets dying. Being murdered. I shrank back. My whole world revolved around being inside where it was safe and warm. The mysterious outside could only be filled with darkness and killers.

My stomach knotted. Something had to be done to rescue the girl.

I merely felt ~~a deep-seated and growing~~ mild concern for Signey. Thank goodness that wasn't the same thing as caring about her.

Right?

RIGHT?!

Chapter 17

MISTAKE NUMBER TWO: never take matters into your own paws. Let someone else get their hands dirty.

I marched out into the hallway. Had it ever been this dark before? Bravery rose up ~~wanted to throw up~~ within me.

I tiptoed past Stuart's nursery. I couldn't help but imagine that even in his sleep he continued to stare at me.

I even made it to the bathroom door without getting mugged. Thank you to whoever installed the little night-light near the toothbrushes. Not that I am afraid of the dark, mind you. I'm just saying . . .

Mother and Father's door loomed ahead. I inched forward.

But what if Signey's parents kept it closed? Fair enough. That would be the end of the road, wouldn't it? Then I could honestly say that I had done all that I could and no more. Had I not already gone over and above the call of duty? Signey was not my responsibility. I could have left her to be eaten by all the ravenous squirrels and rabid chipmunks, but I didn't. Note that. I could go back to sleep and—

Their door sat open a crack. Blast it all!

I rammed their door all the way open with my head.

Why was I the one doing this?! Why not Fred? Just because he didn't have legs didn't give him a good excuse.

I inched closer to the bed. Body parts poked and protruded in every direction off the top of it. Was that snoring?

In all my days living with Madam, I never had to do anything quite so daring as this. Or so stupid.

I jumped up onto the bed. "Oh my word." I clamped a paw over my mouth as quickly as I had said it. I had to thread a minefield. A TV remote here. A Jane Austin book there. Oh, look, a bowl of stale pretzels. A charging cable. So this is where Signey gets it! Slobs, all of them.

I couldn't get anywhere without stepping on something.

I ventured up onto Arthur's chest. (I figured if Ms. Goldborn could call him Arthur, so could I.) Arthur snored like he was taking a chainsaw to one of his award-winning buildings. Thankfully, cats never snore.

At least I don't. ~~Except during naps in the—~~

"Ah, excuse me," I said gently.

Father produced a few HUMPHs and a HERUGH or two, but otherwise didn't stir.

I coughed. "Excuse me."

Mother sat up with her eyes half-closed, grabbed the remote, and mashed a button or two at the TV, which was off already. She flopped back down and rolled over.

May I pause here to say: I do not like to raise my voice. That is not very ladylike, nor is it very civil. A polite lady would *never* scream. Even if the ship was going down, a lady might straighten her dress or ask to have the mustard passed, but *nothing* so vulgar as a scream.

But ugly times call for ugly measures.

"WAKE UP!!!"

Arthur and Mother shot up like lightning had struck.

Signey approached the house, skipping and humming to herself. It felt a little ironic. *Now* she had a spring in her step. Happy-go-lucky. Clearly, she did not know her

121

luck surviving outside for so long. How many mountain lions had just missed her?

Signey talked to herself as she climbed up the latticework. "Oh, Signey, your Valentine moved me. You write so well, far better than that Becky character. When I read it, it made my heart skip a—"

Signey looked up into her open window.

And saw me. Waiting there. Tapping a paw on the sill.

Oh, and Arthur and Mother behind me ~~a minor detail~~.

You should have seen the look that came over Signey's face. The sudden dismay. The dread. I'm sure I gave an impressively stern look that inspired her reaction.

After Signey climbed safely back inside, her parents pointed a lot of fingers. "How could you do this to us?" Mom yelled at Signey. "You could have gotten kidnapped or hurt!"

"Exactly my point," I added.

"Signey, what were you thinking?"

Signey opened her mouth, but nothing came out.

"She clearly *wasn't* thinking," I said as I marched around the convict.

"We are grounding you," Mother said. "For the next week, you will—"

"One week?!" I didn't mean to interrupt. "Excuse me, but isn't one week going a little gentle on her?"

Arthur spoke up. "I think an offense of this caliber requires being grounded for the whole month."

"That's more like it," I said. I liked Arthur. I could see why Ms. Goldborn would choose him to design her next—

Mother interrupted. "Thanks to Kimberly, we found out that you were missing."

Yes, Mother used *my* name. I thought I had made it very clear that they should say an *anonymous source* had notified them. I did not like Mother.

123

Signey turned her gaze to little old *moi*. *Moi* means "me" in French ~~innocently enough~~.

"Wait. I can explain everything," I started.

Signey's eyes narrowed. Narrow like those of a snake in the grass.

"I did it for your own protection, you understand? For your own good." I backed up. "Now might be a good time to go get a snack in the kitchen, yes? Understand, if I hadn't woken up your parents, you might have become a midnight snack yourself! I don't know, eaten by moths, huh?"

Signey's face broke into a smile.

No, *a grin*. A wicked, evil, no-good grin. A dark seed of an idea must have crept into that girl's mind and taken root there. I could have been wrong, of course. Maybe the girl liked to smile at odd times. What did I know?

But I had a hunch. Thanks to my superior upbringing and wisdom, I believed Signey's wicked idea involved *moi*.

BEWARE!

Chapter 18

MISTAKE NUMBER THREE: it's never over until the fat lady meows.

The lights were out in Signey's bedroom. All except for what the moon kindly provided. My bed begged me to return. And as willing as I was to minister to it, I kept one eye open.

Or tried to.

Staying awake is not a cat's specialty. Unless there is a red laser dot on the wall or something. But if my eyes closed, something bad would happen. I could smell it.

Fred snorted and blew a bubble or two. "Me and the boys, we . . ." Fred talked in his sleep. "We aren't making progress . . ."

But my focus remained vigilant on the other one. Signey. She lay in her bed "asleep." Along with heavy breathing, her mouth hung partway open. Drool slowly meandered down one cheek.

Everything seemed fine. Or was that what she wanted me to believe?

Must.

Stay.

Awake . . .

When my eyes finally closed, I dreamed that one of Signey's eyes opened. I dreamed that the crafty girl wiped off the carefully planted drool and sat up. I dreamed that she slipped one leg out from her covers. Then the next. And step after step, she approached me, wearing the same twisted grin I had seen before.

That's when I knew that I hadn't been dreaming.

Signey grabbed me, yanking me out of my bed.

"I once believed that I had a nice cat for a pet," Signey hissed into my ear. She began to smuggle me downstairs. "But now I see that I have a big rat!"

When I went to scream bloody murder (which is perfectly appropriate for a lady to do in *this* kind of circumstance), Signey clamped her hand over my mouth. I clawed and scratched but I batted only air.

Signey surveyed the living room. She slinked over to the front door and opened it.

"I wish I never took you home, Kimberly. Good riddance!"

And with that, she tossed me onto the front porch welcome mat.

"Ha ha. OK. Funny joke," I said. "I am sure that you will look back one day on what I did and recognize the value of—"

KR-CLICK! The door closed.

Wait, did she just lock the door? No. No, there was no way that that girl had just locked the door. She was going to unlock it, right?

"Hello?" I called out. "You're going to unlock the door now, yes?"

I heard crickets. Frogs.

Why wasn't that ungrateful girl unlocking the door?

I mean, why wasn't that ungrateful, no-good child unlocking the door right NOW?! I scratched at the door.

The sounds of nature moved in on me. Hungry.

"Is it getting hot out here or is it just me?" I said, trying to be polite to a tiny bug whose backside was on fire. It flapped closer to me with clear evil in mind.

I tiptoed around it.

Lifting my nose in the air, I stated, "Fine. I don't care." I marched off the patio and down the walkway. If this tactic didn't tug at that girl's heartstrings, then she had a lump of coal for a heart. "I never wanted you to adopt me anyways." I added a sniff for effect.

VROOM! A car zoomed past. I ~~screamed~~ jumped.

Had it swerved out of its way to run me over?!

No Signey.

Alright, I was on my own. I knew right then what to do. The thought of my idea gave me a surge of warmth and fuzzies. My plan made me feel like I could take on anything that attacked me.

I hesitated. Up ahead, in the crack of the sidewalk, a dandelion waited to jump me.

No fear. I was going home!

Why do dogs get all the sniffing power? You can give a mangy dog an old sneaker and sure enough, he will track down where it came from. As disgusting as sniffing an old sneaker would be, mind you.

Not cats.

Cats have power, though.

A sense for house property values.

Show me two houses, and I can tell you which one costs more. It's a gift. Most cats have this ability ~~to a lesser degree than mine, of course~~. Our skill commonly plays out inside the house. For example, we can determine which sofa is the most expensive. That way, we can pick the quality one to cough up our hairballs on.

I had no idea where Madam's mansion was. But when I wandered through the neighborhood, I followed the rich houses. The nicer the houses got, the closer I got to Madam.

I figured that if I walked far enough and long enough, I could find my old life again.

Surely Madam must be awake by now.

To be honest, I didn't think I would make it as far as I did. Maybe the chipmunk gangs had the night off?

I walked and walked. It felt like I walked all night.

But at long last, I saw it!

The mighty iron gates towered before me. Only now, one gate hung to the side, bent. The other gate was missing completely.

The Greek gods and goddesses among the hedges looked fat and lumpy ~~like Fred~~. Why did the gardener not trim the topiary? If Madam saw this, she would throw a fit.

A thick, rusty chain barred the front door. How could any of the servants get in or out? I slipped into the mansion between a pair of loose boards.

Moonlight illuminated the giant foyer. The floors had lost their shine. Dried leaves collected in piles.

"I'm home!" My voice echoed off the empty walls. Taking a paw, I swiped the stairs. Dust lay heavy all around. Madam would fire someone for missing that.

A drip in the kitchen ceiling pooled into a small lake on the floor.

"Hello," I called again. "I'm ready for my breakfast, now."

A pigeon cooed in the distance.

I exited through a broken window onto the back terrace. The tall ornamental grasses lay in piles, damp and decaying. An earthworm tried to jump me, but I was too quick for it.

Why would Madam not have had this cleaned up? Everything lay in shambles. Ruined. Dead.

And when did Taco Bell move into our backyard?

And a trailer park?

Remember when I told you that dogs have great sniffing powers? Well, one of those mangy creatures, a Doberman, must have smelled me. It barked and barked at me, hurting my blessed ears.

The giant creature scraped at the ground beside a trailer home and pulled, straining at its chain. It pulled hard enough to nearly choke itself. ~~Dumb brute.~~

I smiled politely. "Hmm, maybe you should pull harder," I said. "You know . . . finish the job."

I don't know what caused me to say it. I hadn't slept. I could not think straight. My old home was gone. Gone-gone. Where else could I go?

The blasted Doberman continued to bark at me.

I know it wasn't ladylike, but I stuck out my tongue at it.

That's when the Doberman's chain snapped.

Chapter 19

THE DOBERMAN BOUNDED toward me.

His demon eyes were fixed on me like . . . well, like Stuart's. Except the Doberman didn't suck his first four fingers.

I stepped back. Was there any chance the Doberman had been barking at the earthworm?

I was a goner. I knew it. The ship *was* going down, *and* I was about to be murdered. Yet I did not cry out. I calmly licked a paw and began cleaning my face. The least I could do was look presentable.

The hound of hell was nearly upon me when—

"BACK OFF, BUSTER!"

Signey leaped in front of me. "THIS IS MY CAT! AND YOU CAN'T HAVE HER!" She roared as fierce as a ~~moth~~ lion.

The Doberman tucked its tail—YELP YELP YELP!—and ran. Scaredy cat.

But a new fear entered me. Signey had been angry with me. Like, you-knocked-over-the-Tiffany-lamp angry. What if she had spared me from the dumb dog only to kill me herself? I wouldn't blame her. Not for what I did. Ratting her out to her parents wasn't very lady—

"Kimberly," Signey said, throwing herself down on her knees before me. Her voice was little more than a whisper. "I am sooo sorry, Kimberly. I am so, so sorry."

Signey reached out and—

Hugged me.

Tight.

Her eyes clamped shut. She squeezed and squeezed me, rocking side to side.

I should say, I had never received a hug before that. Not like that. I didn't know how to take it. What did it all mean?

A part of me melted like butter. Another part of me stayed resistant in case the harsh lectures came next. But that hug lasted. We were together in each other's arms. I wanted to give myself over to it fully, but I didn't dare. This was something new. I didn't have a name for it. It wasn't like gold and diamonds. Yet somehow it almost felt more costly. More extravagant.

But how could that be? This girl did not have money. Compared to Madam, Signey was dirt-poor.

Exhaustion began to take over.

I brushed away all my crazy thoughts and questions as Signey carried me to Rhonda the Honda. Apparently,

Arthur and Mother had tracked me with my GPS collar.
Go figure.

As the sun rose that morning, Signey and I were both
desperate for some much-needed sleep. She again invited
me to share her bed. She even cleaned it and put on new
sheets, just for me.

Oddly, Signey knelt before her bed and folded her
hands. "Dear Jesus, please forgive me for treating Kimberly so badly tonight. I was terrible and what I did is
nearly unforgivable."

At least she got that right.

Signey continued. "Thank you for your forgiveness.
And if you would, let sweet Kimberly forgive me as well."

Well, I would have to see about that. I hadn't yet come
up with the appropriate punishment for such a heinous
crime, but I was confident that I would think of something.

Exhausted, we both dropped arm in paw into Signey's bed.

Signey whispered in my ear, "I wouldn't trade this for the world."

Weeks later, I dug around in Signey's closet. I needed a good pair of shoes that I could sharpen my claws on ~~destroy~~.

"What about these fuzzy unicorn slip-ons?" I asked Signey. "You are done with those hideous things by now, surely."

No response.

"I'm supposed to take your silence as a yes, right?"

More quiet.

"Signey, listen. Can we focus here?" I looked around the corner. "I've got the itch and if I don't do something right this instant—"

I found her. Signey stood before the full-length mirror that hung on the back of her bedroom door. Using both hands, she squeezed in her waist while sucking in her cheeks. She turned back and forth, checking her profile.

"Uh, can we get back to the fuzzy unicorn slip-ons? What are you doing? Are you alright?"

"Kimberly, do you think I'm fat?"

"Fat? Girl, you are as healthy as a—"

"I overheard Kelly in second period Spanish say that Jimmy Bolen doesn't like fat girls."

In case you've been wondering, Jimmy Bolen, or "Jimmy the Jerk" as he became known, had taken Signey's valentine into school. And for a laugh, he passed it around the boy's locker room.

"If you really want my opinion, Signey, I think Kelly needs to shut her big, fat mouth, if you ask—"

Signey walked out of the room.

I followed. "Signey, listen to me . . ."

Where did she go? The bathroom?

By the time I got in there, Signey had the digital scale out. She stepped onto it.

And cringed.

"Signey, I somehow do not think that Jimmy Bowl-head—or whatever his name is—is really the kid you want to be taking health tips from."

Signey stared in the bathroom mirror. She pushed against the skin underneath her chin, making her neck seem taller, leaner.

"Hey, look," I said. "A bathtub! Wanna take a bath instead?"

Signey sucked in her gut and nearly disappeared—the poor thing.

"Wanna give me a bath?"

Signey tightened her belt two more notches. And winced.

"That was a joke. Get it? Haha. OK, no really . . . I'm getting concerned."

Signey sighed.

At dinner that night, Signey continued her shenanigans. I watched her. I had a front row seat. Under the table, of course.

Her hand would slip down from above. First, part of a chicken breast "drifted" down into her napkin—how convenient. Then more chicken and a few string beans arrived. A regular conveyor belt of food continued to accumulate in her paper napkin. If it held much more, the napkin would burst. Was no one else seeing this?

I leaped up onto an empty seat near Mother.

"Hello? Parents?" I interrupted. "Can we talk about the kitchen faucet problem later?"

"Oh, hello, Kimberly," Mother said. "Are you hungry? Were you fed tonight?"

"Um, yes, thank you." I nodded my head in the direction of Signey. "Looks like someone else is not very hungry, though. Catch my drift. Huh? Huh?!"

"But it continues to spray out the side of the handle when I turn on the hot water."

The woman was daft. I still didn't like her.

I turned to Stuart.

No, I did not *want* to turn to Stuart. I could already feel his eyes drilling into ~~my soul~~ me. That little devil.

I craned my neck to see over him. "Arthur, my good man. Look at your daughter."

"Honey, I'd be glad to look at the faucet, but plumbing's not my specialty. I'd probably only make the leak worse."

I jumped back down to the floor.

The napkin bulged even greater. Had she stuffed it with a second helping?

"May I be excused?" Signey asked. "I have homework to do."

Liar. I could not wait to see her smuggle that football out into the kitchen.

"Yes, you may, dear," her mother said. "Maybe I should look at the leak. I bet I could fix it."

No! They were not paying attention. Signey nearly made it out the door.

So, I did what any self-respecting parent would do if their kitchen faucet was not leaking.

I jumped in between Signey's feet.

Chapter 20

ANOTHER CAT SKILL is to get underfoot. Usually we have no need for it, so we stay clear. But when it serves our purposes, it is a useful skill to master.

The goal was to trip Signey so that she'd spill her bloated napkin. Of course, there would be a mess. A giant one. And then her parents would see her trickery.

But things rarely go according to plan.

First of all, Signey needs to go back to wearing her fuzzy unicorn slip-ons. Was she wearing army boots? Whatever. It felt like getting kicked by a mule.

I went flying.

Signey didn't even stumble.

Now I knew what it had felt like for Fred to go flying. Only I did not like it. Not one bit.

I somersaulted into the kitchen and landed with complete grace and agility like a ballerina. OK, I would have, but I got disoriented. I could have sworn the ceiling swapped places with the floor. Doesn't matter.

I ended up in the kitchen trash can. Ugh! Who actually throws away such ugly trash? And as a side note: the Taylors ate entirely too much yogurt. Or, for that matter, threw away too much yogurt. It smelled sour and twisted.

But no one looked at Signey or noticed what she had smuggled out of the room. Nobody even questioned why she went outside suddenly and visited the trash bins. And nobody saw the wounded girl who dumped her perfectly good dinner there.

Signey and I battled at almost every meal. She skimped and pushed food away. I tipped over the bowl of oranges so they rolled into her lap. Each of us knew what the other was doing. It became a war that no one won.

And whom could I talk to about it? I had nobody.

OK, I had Fred, but I'm not sure he counts.

Fine. Fred counts.

I went to talk with him. "Hey, Fred, have you noticed how tired Signey is lately?"

Fred stopped his digging as I approached.

"Tired, you say? Yes." He wiped his brow and took a breather. "Me and the boys have been more tired these days. Thanks for askin'."

"I mean, I went on a hunger strike when I arrived here. But that was different, you know? That and I had more in reserve, if you catch my drift. Actually, forget I said that. But have you seen Signey? She's as skinny as a rail."

"I know what you mean," Fred said. "We fill up one pail and then another. It's endless work, really. I'm starting to wonder if we'll ever escape."

I suddenly realized something. I marched over to the other side of the dresser and looked down. "She's not eating cheese curls anymore. You notice, Fred? Where are the hidden stashes? You know there's a problem if there are no Real™ cheese curls around! Not that they are *real* to begin with . . ."

"A problem, you say?" Fred sighed. "We used to think we were making progress, but now I'm not so sure. We keep digging but it feels like there's no bottom. You ever wonder if you're merely digging the same ground? You know, over and over?"

I paced back to Fred's bowl. "Over and over, I tried to tell her parents, but they aren't listening. No one listens. Everything is about that blasted kitchen faucet. Blah, blah, blah."

"I hear you," Fred said. He slumped down to the bottom of his bowl. "I'm depressed."

The strength left my legs. I seemed to melt myself. What was wrong with that girl?

Now, don't get me wrong. I was NOT starting to care. I merely didn't want a nice girl to go and throw it all away merely because she could not see her own beauty.

That's all.

Signey walked in and flopped on her bed.

Instantly I saw what needed to be done. I jumped down to the bed and climbed onto Signey's chest. One of the best ways to motivate someone is to get right in their face and lecture them. Watch and learn.

"Signey, listen up, girlfriend!" I used the word "girlfriend" to show her that I was on the same level. You know, one of her "kind."

"Kimberly, I'm too tired to play." She pushed me away. "I just want to sleep."

I got right back in her face. "And do you know WHY you are so tired? It is because of the Keebler elves." I did not know exactly where I was going with this, but I had seen something about it on TV once. "If you do not eat properly and send good food down into your belly, then the Keebler elves don't have anything to make cookies with. And if the elves are not able to make any cookies . . ." I was a little fuzzy about this next part, but I did not let on. "Well, then think about all the little children in the world who . . . who won't have cookies in their lunchboxes. Yes, that's right!"

Signey rolled away from me. Did she already know how digestion worked?

I turned away. What else could I do?

I caught a glimpse of myself in her full-length mirror.

My first thought was that the blasted mirror was one of the problems!

Actually, to be honest, that was the second thing. My first thought was, "Look at that gorgeous cat. I wonder who does her nails?"

I jumped off the bed and approached the tall mirror.

Signey had wedged magazine clippings into its frame. Images of thin ladies with big lips. Fragile figures who all frowned ~~and wore too much pink~~. Lean women who stared back with ghostly eyes.

I clawed at one photo. It fell off the mirror and floated to the floor.

SCHWING! Out came the claws. I had confetti before me in a matter of seconds.

I clawed at more images. A few fell but the majority were out of my reach. I looked back at Signey on her bed. She lay curled up like a baby.

I turned back to ~~my nemesis~~ the mirror.

BNNT! I rammed it with my head.

A few more images drifted to the floor.

BNNT! BNNT!

Images began falling like autumn leaves.

BNNT! BNN—

I heard a new sound. It went more like SKEERT!

~~Can someone check my spelling on that?~~

The mirror wobbled and began to sway. My highly tuned senses told me this might be a good time to—

The nail that held the mirror pulled out of the door.

I jumped for dear life.

Chapter 21

CRASHHH!

The mirror shattered on the ground. Shards of glass skated across the floor, radiating out from the impact.

Signey jolted up. "Kimberly, are you alright?"

"Um . . . I think so."

Signey and I gingerly approached the remains. The glass fragments distorted the models' photos underneath. Their faces became twisted and bent. I laughed.

Was Signey mad at me for what I had done? I couldn't tell.

Signey carefully reached between the shards for a magazine clipping. When she lifted it, the page caught on the glass and tore in half. She held up a picture of a now-headless model. Looking around, she matched it with the head of a model that had survived my claws.

"Look, Kim."

The new figure's head was twice the size it should be for the size of its new body. I wanted to laugh again, but I still didn't know what Signey was feeling. I frowned instead.

"Look at this one." Signey had ripped another magazine clipping. A new head sat on a new body. It didn't fit at all.

"Ha!" I fake-laughed, not wanting to look too excited. But it really was funny.

Signey grabbed a pair of scissors and made several new Frankenstein models. Holding another head onto a different body, she made the model talk with a funny voice. "Hi there. My name is Victoria. Do you think I'm beautiful? Maybe I should give up modeling."

I noticed Signey smile.

She pulled down her headless sports trophies and tried a few more heads on them before sweeping up the glass and magazine clippings. It all went into the trash.

She led me to the kitchen, where she began cutting up fresh strawberries. She even put some in my food bowl.

Signey lay on the floor beside me. She had a bowl of strawberries for herself. She picked from them, licking the juice off her fingers after each one.

A part of me wanted to tell her that wasn't very lady-like, but I held my tongue.

We ate in silence.

Together.

The morning of Signey's twelfth birthday started off with a very loud and very annoying beeping sound outside. And MUCH too early. What—it was only 1:00 p.m.?!

A large and smelly rental truck backed into the Taylors' yard.

From a window, I watched them unload. First, they hoisted up a big, white tent, hammering in the posts and running the lines. Signey's parents must have rented a bouncy house ~~can someone say "tacky"?~~ too. I watched it grow from a small, white block into a perky, overstuffed balloon. I wondered what my claws could do to that.

Signey's cousin arrived early and set up big boxes on poles. Ugly cables streamed from them all over the lawn. And when she turned the whole contraption on, it sounded like the world was coming to an end. What kind of music are kids listening to these days?! Too much THUMP THUMP THUMP.

The Taylors' guests started to arrive. They had strict instructions to stay out of the house, except for the use of the bathrooms. I was pleased.

There were a lot of hugs and a lot of little cousins with runny noses. Did everyone from Norway have blond hair and freckles? Either way, it looked like they needed a lot of sunblock.

Someone placed a homemade crown on Signey's head. Paper, mind you. Nothing expensive. But she didn't seem embarrassed. Peculiar.

And the food. Signey's parents didn't hire a five-star caterer or any waitstaff. For that matter, Mother and Arthur provided the birthday cake and the ~~disgusting-colored~~ punch. That was it. But the aunts and uncles brought more food than an entire polo team could eat. In Tupperware containers of every shape and size it came. In heaps and mounds. Most of it I did not recognize because it was—how do I say it?—beneath standards. You know, potato chips, coleslaw . . .

But someone else must have brought the good stuff: seafood! I pressed both of my front paws up against the window. Giant platters of steaming shrimp and lobster trimmed with lemon corkscrews took center stage. Oh! To merely nibble from those scraps would be a delight.

The gift table overflowed as well. Presents piled so high that they pushed up the tree branches above the table. More gifts littered the ground underneath.

A cotton candy machine was running, and something that had been hooked up to a garden hose. I don't know if you will believe me, but kids actually ran and fell onto it. It acted like ice. They went flying along the ground at unhealthy speeds, only to crash into a giant ~~bacteria-filled~~ puddle at the end of it. I was sure it was only a matter of time before someone got hurt.

But something else gnawed at me.

I could not understand why everyone seemed to be enjoying themselves. They appeared to be experiencing a kind of pleasure I was unfamiliar with. There were more smiles than potato salad—if you can believe that. And the laughter . . .

It almost made me want to join in.

Almost.

When Madam threw a party, she did it with class. The backyard of the mansion transformed into a scene from an opera. There were crystal champagne flutes, sparkling chandeliers, and the Elizabethan chairs pulled out of storage. But I do not remember anyone enjoying themselves half as much as the people at this party.

For that matter, Madam never laughed. Not even once. It wasn't proper.

In the backyard, I watched as Arthur and Mother danced close together under the string lights. Even though the music thumped on, they danced slowly. Like they were listening to their own song. They looked into each other's eyes. They stood so close there seemed to be magic or something between them.

At the entrance to the bouncy house sat a bucket of spray cans. Everyone who entered grabbed one. They kept pointing the cans at each other. Dare I say it looked like colored string shot out from the cans? It littered the inside of the bouncy house like a rainbow had ~~barfed~~ fallen. The screams and laughter continued. Were the kids honestly enjoying this? How could they when no one wore helmets or eye protection?

That's when I saw Signey sneaking toward her own house . . . and me. She crept forward with something hidden in her arms, tucked under a mound of paper napkins. Signey looked around to see if anyone watched.

What had that girl done now? And why was she acting like a thief?

By the size of that girl's grin, she must have stolen the Crown Jewels.

Chapter 22

THE BACK DOOR to the Taylors' house creaked open.

"Kimberly!" Signey whispered as she slipped inside.

I marched over to confront her. I had prepared a rather lengthy reprimand for the impish girl and was preparing my best stern face when she slid a plate onto the floor in front of me.

"Shhh. I smuggled you a surprise, Kimberly."

I could smell it before I could see it. My nose twerked. No. No, it couldn't be. My senses surely were teasing me—playing tricks!

Signey yanked off the napkins.

Shrimp!

The entire plate brimmed with the beautiful, orange, ~~not pink!~~ plump, succulent food of the gods.

"It's all for you, girl," Signey said as she set down her own plate next to mine. It was no surprise what filled Signey's plate. Not-real Real™ cheese curls. How odd that both plates mirrored each other. Both were covered with orange, curly shapes. One clearly a gift from heaven and the other from . . . well, you know . . . the other place.

WHAT A GIFT! That girl, for all her poverty, sure knew how to give handsomely. And on her own birthday, no less. Had I misjudged Signey all along? Was there more to her gifts than I had given her credit for?

Ohhh, the mouthwatering, delectable, succulent, sweetly organic, straight-from-the-ocean beauty of it all! The smell alone—with that dash of Old Bay—made me nearly faint from sheer, euphoric pleasure. Angels strummed on golden harps. Order had returned to the universe and—

The back door banged open. Probably someone trying to find the bathroom. But it wasn't. I heard Arthur's voice. He spoke with someone on his cell as he entered.

"Yes, I have finished the plans, but today is NOT a good day to pick them—"

"Now, Arthur, I am simply going to pop over there since I'm in the neighborhood."

I recognized the voice on the other end of the call instantly. My eyes shot open. A surge of electricity ran through my body. Every hair in my ~~long, sleek, and skinny~~ body stood up.

Ms. Goldborn!

"I need those plans, darling. You cannot possibly have something more important going on."

Arthur clamped a hand over the phone and spun to Signey. "You need to get back out to your guests, Signey."

"Yes, Dad," Signey said with a wink aimed at me. She went to yank her own plate away, but in the process bumped mine. I must have been the only one to see it: a single shrimp fell off my plate. It landed on Signey's plate. One orange curl in a sea of orange curls.

"Wait, Signey!" I cried. "Did you see what fell—"

But Signey exited the house, skipping back to her party, oblivious.

What could I do? Should I run after her? The door was now closed. How could I warn her and—

"It is my daughter's twelfth birthday today," Arthur said, interrupting my thoughts. He was trying so hard to be firm. Poor man. He clearly didn't know the force behind a wealthy lady who wanted something. "I will not let you interrupt her—"

"Oh, that's precious," Ms. Goldborn broke in. "I shall be right over."

"NO!" Arthur exclaimed, but he was too late. Ms. Goldborn had already hung up. He slapped his forehead and ran into his home office.

I froze. Before me lay the most beautiful spread of delectables that had graced the Taylors' house. On the other hand, my chance to escape was mere seconds away. And who was going to warn Signey about the shrimp-of-most-certain-doom that lay on her plate?

ACK! What to do, what to do?! I wanted to scream. I wanted to melt. I wanted—

And then it came to me. I knew instantly what to do. I had it programmed inside of me from Day One when I arrived at the Taylors' house.

I sprinted for the bedroom and jumped up onto Signey's dresser. "Fred, I want to say goodbye."

"Goodbye?" Fred poked his head out from behind the plastic castle, a pink stone falling from his lips. "Blimey. 'Ave you found a way to escape?"

"I have, Fred," I said as clearly as I could, but something went wrong with my throat. It felt like something had squeezed it. "Tell the boys—I wish them well." What was happening to me?! Freedom awaited, and now I could barely talk. "Best of luck with the digging. I wish I could take you—I mean *all of you*—with me."

Fred snapped to attention and raised a fin in one final salute.

I had to turn away. My eyes had problems ~~were leaking~~.

DING DONG!

I raced to the living room and dashed behind the potted hibiscus. Arthur opened the front door. Ms. Goldborn pushed him aside and strutted inside, tugging at her long, white gloves.

"Hello, Arthur, dear." She ran a long fingernail along his cheek. "Thank you for making this appointment. I'm sure we can both agree that this is a *little* more important than a silly birthday party, no?" She looked more stunning than ever with her cream-white silk dress and heels.

Ms. Goldborn stepped into the office with Arthur fumbling behind, his arms full of cardboard tubes.

The front door yawned open a crack.

WHAT SHOULD I DO?! About a million ~~neon emotions~~ clear, logical thoughts flooded my mind. THIS WAS WHAT I WANTED!!! What I had always wanted! My ONE chance to escape.

I also really had to pee. I don't know if you needed to know that but—

ESCAPE WAS NOW OR NEVER!

Chapter 23

So I LEFT.

And that is my story.

Which brings me back to the here and now. And to this amazing smell! The hand-stitched leather. Ohhh, the luxury and quality of Rolls-Royce. It smells like . . .

. . . money!

I strut back and forth across the glorious back seat with my head held high, the imaginary cameras desperate for another photo of me. After all my trials and suffering, the Rolls is *mine* now. How could it get any better than this? Finally, I'm happy! I am. Don't I deserve to be happy? I can't contain how happy I am right now. I'm spilling over with true peace and inner—

Except I'm not.

In my rush to get out of the Taylors' house, I had forgotten that nagging feeling. But now it's back. Like I'm forgetting something—leaving something behind. But what? Nothing can possibly be that important.

The heaping plate of shrimp? I didn't even get to eat one. No, no, that's silly. Surely Ms. Goldborn will have plenty more shrimp, right?

Maybe it's that glorious cardboard box—my bed. What if Ms. Goldborn's expensive beds aren't as comfortable? Or snug? Oh come on, Kimberly, surely a lady this rich has the very best beds. Yes, yes.

The mac and cheese? What if I can't survive without that blessed mac and cheese? And Petcare—oh, dear—

and being the queen of Sheba. And that stupid, idiotic goldfish digging in his stupid bowl!

"AHHH!" I scream. "Why is it SO DIFFICULT to leave?!"

"Why, hello, deary."

I jump. The sound of a real voice unnerves me.

"And who are you, precious?" asks Ms. Goldborn, a roll of plans clutched in her ~~claw~~ hand. Her diamond rings blind me in the evening light. Ms. Goldborn climbs into the driver's seat and shuts the door. "Aren't you a beautiful thing," she says, grinning at me.

I try to breathe. Can't.

Ms. Goldborn runs a fingernail across my cheek. "You look like you could use a good home, no? I know of one. A new one, about to be built from Italian marble and expensive cedarwood. Come live with me." Ms. Goldborn leans in close to me. I can feel the heat on her sweet, artificial breath. "I will make sure you are spoiled like you have *never* been before!"

Our eyes lock. Soul to soul.

"*Spoiled*," she said. Just hearing that word again brings clarity back. Crystalline focus.

Ms. Goldborn grins and grabs hold of the keys in the ignition. She twists them. The car purrs to life. My happiness returns. These good feelings and deep-seated joy are here to stay, I can tell.

Ms. Goldborn shifts the Rolls into gear.

Finally, I can truly sit back and relax. I've done it! I am back in the life of riches. Minks and pearls will be my new playthings—my new friends. I shall have no more worries in this happy, happy world. None.

The car lurches forward. It rattles my nerves. Why?

Scanning the windows, I can see that we are leaving the Taylors' house. Goodbye, and good riddance! I laugh, loud and maniacal. Leaving makes me even happier, if that's possible. I am the happiest happier I have ever been. Almost like happiness itself is giving me a big, fat hug and—

A hug.

THE hug.

Memories of Signey's hug suddenly wrap around me like one of those warm towels straight from the dryer. That amazing, yet calming, Hope Diamond kind of hug. And suddenly I get it.

I see.

I understand Signey. Her riches. She *had* touched me, infected me, inside and out. And it was glorious! All the gold and diamonds in the world weren't worth what Signey had given me. That simple hug. It *was* the most valuable thing I have ever known. I wanted more. I NEEDED IT! That's what I had left behind. I was leaving that hug. Leaving that touch. Leaving Signey.

WHAT.

HAVE.

I.

DONE?!

"I'm . . . I'm sorry," I calmly say, wiping an eye ~~since~~ ~~someone must be cutting onions nearby~~. I clear my throat and regain composure. "I have made a grave mistake. I should not be here in your car. Kindly let me out."

Ms. Goldborn does not hear me, or she refuses to stop.

"Wait, please. No, no, no. We cannot leave. I mean, I CAN NOT LEAVE!"

The Taylors' hydrangeas whiz past, then the Taylors' birdbath, and the Taylors' mailbox. We're heading out onto the main street. Why won't this old witch stop?!

I push on my door. It's closed tight. I run across the back seat and ~~headbutt~~ try the other door. A wall of steel. I vow that this vehicle will not become my new prison.

More than anything right now I need air. I can't breathe. OK, correction, I need air *and* Ms. Goldborn to stop the car. No, actually, I need air, Ms. Goldborn to stop, and a litter box because I still have to pee like a—never mind. That's not very ladylike.

Desperate times call for desperate cats. I crouch down, whisper a prayer, and then I—

Let me be clear here: it is one thing to observe proper behavior in certain times of crisis, as we have already discussed. But there are other times that are simply outside the strict rules and codes of behavior. Like now! Got it? I do not want you to think poorly of me for what I am about to do.

I leap onto Ms. Goldborn's head.

"AAAAGH! What are you doing, cat?!"

I really did not know what to expect from Ms. Goldborn. I can tell you that I did NOT expect her to thrash her head about so much. That of course only makes me grab tighter. Along with screams of treason and bloody murder, her hands fly off the wheel, clawing at me.

The car swerves side to side like a toy boat in a storm.

KCHUNK! And there rip out the neighbor's boxwood shrubs. I grip tighter. KTHUNK! There splinters a mailbox.

I look up. I honestly cannot imagine the upcoming thick oak tree will actually give way to our—KR-CRUNCH!

Yes, I like it when I am right.

But how did I end up on the back seat again? And why is Ms. Goldborn playing with a big, white balloon in her lap?

"This is no time to play!" I say indignantly. "There is a sweet and lovely girl to save! MY sweet and lovely girl!"

Most of my side window is now gone. I leap out over the splintered remains.

Ms. Goldborn throws open her door. Her hair points in every direction except nice. ~~That isn't a wig, is it?~~ A part of her dress hangs, ripped. She teeters on one broken heel.

I am not sure I need to point this out, but her tone of voice is not very . . . well, I'll let you decide.

"YOU. DIRTY. ROTTEN. CREATURE!" Ms. Goldborn breathes heavily. "You come back here this IN-STANT!"

I sprint away with a big, angry gorilla in pursuit.

Sorry. That's not a very nice thing to say.

I take leave of the car with a big, angry gorilla in pursuit.

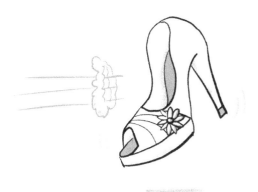

Chapter 24

I NEED TO pick up the pace. Ms. Goldborn looks serious. Like she could do serious damage if she got her well-manicured nails around my throat.

Between naps and eating, running has never been one of my hobbies.

I race away from the steaming car. Maybe ten or twenty miles? Trust me, fifty yards feels that far.

Side stitch! Cramp, cramp.

But what if Signey is already flailing on the ground? What if she is clutching her own throat ~~with those horribly bitten fingernails~~ unable to breathe?

I understand now. That girl didn't have money, yet she was rich. She had given me everything. Herself. All of it. She spoiled me, and I walked away. Like overlooking a Van Gogh at a yard sale.

I shove dignity to the side. And run!

Of course, the sprinkler system on this side of the house tries to ambush me. I dodge and weave. Not one drop lands on me.

Ms. Goldborn, on the other hand, hits the first puddle and vaults into the air. Up goes her $4,000 remaining heel. Down goes her ~~butt~~ derrière. SPLOOSH!

"AHHH! My Oscar de la Renta!" she yells like it is a swear word.

The backyard party opens up before me.

I have to pause. It is overwhelming. The people. The activities. It's too much. And a new thought overtakes me. Does returning mean more of Mother's lipstick and baths and—I'm not sure I can do this.

Then I see her. Signey is still standing. And still alive, unless she has died standing up. ~~Is that a thing?~~

Ms. Goldborn scrambles back to her feet, water and muck streaming from her. She smears muddy hair away from her eyes. "Where is that MONSTER?!"

Her rage draws gasps from those who are close by. They stare in horror, frozen in place.

I take off toward the bouncy house. I hurdle a pile of ~~smelly and terribly unorganized~~ sneakers and leap up onto the puffy surface. I'm sure you have never gotten into one of these contraptions, but it is like walking on water. Progress proves to be tricky. And it smells weird, like feet.

"Excuse me. Pardon," I say. The small children next to me stop jumping. They turn and watch as I high-step past. One child reaches out to pet me.

"DON'T EVEN THINK ABOUT IT!" I dish out my stern face.

Ms. Goldborn races after me into the bouncy house. She scrambles up onto the unsteady surface, walking like a sailor on deck in rough waves. She is halfway to my side when a greenish color washes over her face. Ms. Goldborn pauses. One hand shoots up and clamps over her mouth. She smiles politely then spins away. It would be inappropriate to mention what happens next, but—oh, I'll let this kid speak for me.

"Mommy, Mommy!" One child bursts into tears, his lower lip quivering. He points a chubby finger toward Ms. Goldborn. "She barfed in the bouncy house! Does that mean we have to get out?"

More people turn to take in the commotion.

I make a vow. If Signey eats that shrimp, then by golly, I will kill her before it does.

Suddenly, a flurry of shiny metal races toward me. I clamp my eyes shut as I prepare to meet my maker. Then a pair of hands gently lifts me from the ground—Terri in her blessed wheelchair! Signey's best friend scoops me up onto her lap. I open my mouth, but before I can say anything, Terri interprets my every need. "You need Signey, don't you, Kimberly?"

I nod, but I don't think Terri even notices. Is it possible to get whiplash while riding in a wheelchair? We race across the yard, dodging various second cousins and weaving between great-aunts. There is no way I could have made it on my own through this many tail stompers.

But then a row of folding chairs blocks our path.

I leap from Terri's lap up onto the food tables. "Terri, how can I thank—"

"Go!" Terri interrupts. "Do what you have to do, Kimberly!"

The food tables stretch out to infinity. I race over the spread, jumping here and there to get closer to Signey. She is lifting another not-real-cheese cheese curl to her mouth. Hello?! Look at your plate, girl!

Like dodging explosives in a minefield, I leap mounds of freakishly colored ambrosia and tater tots, and vats of mashed potato, and au gratin potatoes, and every other dish of potato known to mankind.

I catch a glimpse of Signey's orange fingers. In slow motion, she reaches for the next one.

It is not cheese. No, no—this time I mean that it is *not* a cheese curl!

BOOOOM!!! All heads spin.

As the bouncy house deflates, Ms. Goldborn rises up from within, a shell of her former beauty. As she pries one shoe from its hole in the bouncy house, Ms. Goldborn raises the heel above her head. She screams.

"AAAAGHHH!"

The entire backyard hushes in fright.

"Where is that CAT?!" she hollers, wild-eyed, clutching her remaining heel.

Signey lifts the shrimp. It hovers between plate and mouth.

"NO!" I yell as I crouch low for one last leap. "Signey, STOP!"

Ms. Goldborn spies me. Like Zeus hurling a thunderbolt, Ms. Goldborn throws her spiked shoe. It whirls end over end through the air, directly at me.

The shrimp nearly touches Signey's open lips. Like a defending lioness, I launch.

The spiked weapon screams through the air.

I stretch midair, paw reaching toward Signey, and—

I'm sorry, I *really* must pee.

Is this a bad place to stop?

STRAIGHT FROM THE DRYER!

Chapter 25

OK, FINE. I'll hold it.

The heel misses me and slams into a bowl of ugly pink sherbet punch. The bowl flips and launches a wall of ghastly liquid toward me.

My paw swings upward, straining.

And like the champion tennis player I could be if I wanted to (but I don't), I swat the shrimp from Signey's hand, which was millimeters from her mouth.

At the same time, I get blanketed with the nasty pink sherbet punch. Head to tail. Wet, sticky, foamy, and fizzy. Did I say "wet"? I mean *wet*-wet.

I land on all fours, like a ballerina. A perfect landing as usual, but I am drenched.

The hush over the backyard breaks.

Signey's uncle looks down at the orange curl that landed at his feet. Then he points to me.. "That cat saved your life, Signey! You can't eat shellfish."

The family crowd cheers, but it is interrupted by a roar from Ms. Goldborn.

"I WANT THAT CAT DEAD!"

Signey picks me up. "You will NOT touch my Kimberly!" She cradles me. Shields me.

"I will wring the scrawny neck of that CREATURE!"

Arthur steps between Ms. Goldborn and us. "No!" he shouts with a newfound strength. "You may not come any closer. As a matter of fact, you need to GO!"

Ms. Goldborn screams. Her left eye twitches as she holds back a primal rage.

"Excuse me, ma'am," a stern voice interrupts from the side of the house. A police officer and his female partner stand watching, hands on their weapons. Red and blue lights flicker behind them. "Is that your wrecked car out front?" They approach. "The smoldering wreck that you abandoned?"

"Officers," Ms. Goldborn says, sweet as gold, as she neatens her hair and brushes her dress flat. "You do not understand how that cat has utterly destroyed me and my—"

"You can tell us all about it, after your sobriety test," the female officer interrupts. "Downtown."

The first officer pulls one of Ms. Goldborn's arms and then the other behind her back. CLICK. The handcuffs latch. The police begin to lead her away.

"I won't forget this!" Ms. Goldborn wails over her shoulder. "I won't forget YOU, Kimberly! You *will* see me again. That I PROMISE!"

It has been a very long day. I am tired and don't really care if it's not ladylike. I stick out my tongue.

And with that, Ms. Goldborn is gone.

The family circles around, with me at the center. Not just me—I mean with *Signey* and me at the center.

"Kimberly, you were so brave!"

"Weren't you afraid, Kimberly?"

"What you did was simply amazing!"

The praise goes on and on, but I tune it all out. Instead, I focus on Signey's smile. Actually, I do listen to most of the praise, because how often do you actually get that sort of attention?

I mean, really.

But Signey holds me tight the whole time. She never stops smiling at me.

After yet another bath ~~which I really do vow will be the last one I ever have, so help me God~~, Signey dries me off with a warm towel. Yes, straight from the dryer. Signey looks at me and giggles. What starts as a few smirks breaks into a full belly laugh.

"What is your problem, girl?" I bark.

Signey holds me up in front of the bathroom mirror.

Pink.

I have turned pink from the punch, dyed the worst color in the world! I lick a paw and rub myself. The sherbet dye doesn't come off. It is going to take decades for this blasted color to wash out!

"I love it!" Signey squeals. "I love you, Kimberly."

When we go out to join the party again, they cut the cake. But a few raindrops turn into a steady downpour, and the party moves indoors. Later, as each party guest leaves, they wish Signey a happy birthday.

"I'm glad you didn't get hurt today, Kimberly," Mother says as she offers me a leftover shrimp cocktail. Haven't I always said that I love this lady?

Someone had transported Fred and his bowl to the kitchen table to join in the festivities. He blows a few bubbles and then says, "Let me get this straight. You escaped only to end up right back 'ere?" Fred glances left and right then leans in. "Me and the boys might as well give up diggin' if the world's that small."

Stuart offers me his classic stare and four-finger suck. But then, for the first time, he pulls his fingers out of his mouth. He surprises us all when he speaks his first word. "Kitty."

The rain grows heavier.

KRRCRACK!

Thunder! More lightning arcs across the sky.

I abandon the shrimp and run. I'm zipping back and forth—where could I hide?! Under Signey's bed. That is the best place I can think of.

KRCRACK! BOOM!

I shiver. If only the horrible storm would stop. I feel alone, like I did when I lived with Madam. "Dear God, please, oh please, forget my earlier prayers and . . ." I pause. I almost can't say the words, so I whisper them. "Whatever you do, do NOT give me what I deserve."

Signey's face suddenly appears under the bed. She reaches in and strokes me. And yes, fine, my butt elevator kicks in. Signey gently coaxes me out from my hiding spot. She holds me tight as we sit on her bed.

"Don't worry, Kimberly. I've got you," she whispers in my ear. "You're safe. You're loved."

And I am.

I sit back and let Signey's hug soak in. Deep.

Being royalty, living pampered and spoiled—that's a wonderful thing. But to love and be loved?

I wouldn't trade that for the world!

THE END

More family-friendly books from
Jar of Lightning!

SOAK IN SCRIPTURE WHILE YOU
TRANSCRIBE VERSES FROM THE BIBLE!

Scripture
HANDWRITING
WORKBOOK

In the beginning...

OLD TESTAMENT EDITION

jaroflightning.com

TREASURE HUNT
MAZES™

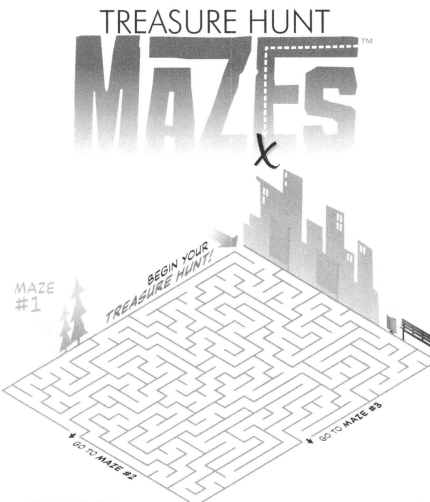

MAZE #1

BEGIN YOUR TREASURE HUNT!

GO TO MAZE #2

GO TO MAZE #3

CHOOSE YOUR OWN
TRAIL!™

In the **Treasure Hunt Mazes™** series, you get all the fun of navigating hundreds of mazes as well as the excitement of picking your own path as you go!

And why not look for
LOST TREASURE
while you're at it?!

INSPIRED BY REAL STORIES OF GOLD AND TREASURE!
Try FREE samples at jaroflightning.com

CRAFT HOLIDAY

CHEER!

CHRISTMAS PAPERCRAFT VILLAGE

JAR OF
Lightning

Leaving a positive review

where you purchased this book
greatly helps authors like Kimberly!

Thank you!

Made in United States
North Haven, CT
04 February 2022